A CAPTIVE STATE

By

Patricia Letourneau Henderson

Mr. Sheenan:
Thank you for your
support —
Pattie Letourneau Henderson
Mar '03

P.S. Please don't hold the "rough"
spots against my parents!!!...

ISBN: 1-4033-8926-8 (e-book)
ISBN: 1-4033-8927-6 (Paperback)
ISBN: 1-4033-8928-4 (Hardcover)

Library of Congress Control Number: 2002095411

This book is printed on acid free paper.

Printed in the United States of America
Bloomington, IN

1stBooks - rev. 11/13/02

Acknowledgments

To my Grandmothers, who were so important to me growing up-I thank you for all the wonderful memories that still make me smile, even though you've been gone a long time now; To my parents, who always told me I could be anything I wanted to be, thanks for letting me take my own time and route getting here; To my brother, thanks for being the person that you are and allowing me to be me; To my sisters, my first readers who didn't tell me to quit my day job, but did ask if they could read anything else I've written-thanks for the encouragement and your friendship; To the Hendersons and Leclercs, thanks for making me a part of your families; To my only "outside" reader, my friend Mary Ann, thank you for always being there for me no matter what; To John and Mark, thanks for letting me try out my stories on you when we were growing up, as well as giving me so much material to work with; To George Chaffee, thanks for taking a chance on me all those years ago; To J. Brady Young, thanks for giving me a second wind; and last, but not least, thank you to my incredible husband, David, and my fantastic children Chelsea and Jared-I couldn't have done any of this without your love and support.

Chapter 1

Samantha Atherton Armstrong was a mystery to those who worked for her, along with anyone else she came into contact with. It hadn't come naturally; but was the result of an elaborate cover cultivated since early childhood.

While Vermont is a place where mysteries have their place in legends and heroes of old, her people do not want them in daily life. Vermonters need to connect everyone they meet to something they are familiar with. To assist with this, all acquaintances are assigned to one of three categories: Real Vermonters (so at the very least related to someone known), Tourists (from some far away place that can be pointed to on a map, while they are told "Don't let us keep you from getting back there as quickly as possible") or Flatlanders (tourists who make the mistake of moving in). A Vermonter will sadly proclaim that he is not a Real Vermonter, since his mother's father's mother's father was actually born in New Hampshire. On the other hand, a Flatlander will proudly announce in a letter to the editor of the local paper that he is practically a Real-Vermonter, since he has lived in his adopted state for almost a decade. Obviously the two don't mix.

When Samantha moved to Burlington in the early eighties to jump on the captive insurance bandwagon, she was greeted with the quiet disgust that most Flatlanders are too ignorant to respect. Some of her foolish associates actually looked on the term as one of endearment, instead of the mark of a pariah that it was intended to be. She understood that while anyone could physically move to this land of enchantment, only a Real Vermonter could share the depths of his soul with the Green Mountains.

The Flatlander label was a double-edged sword for Samantha, because she actually was a Real Vermonter. The saving grace was that she considered herself an outsider anyway, since she hadn't felt any special attachment to the land while growing up.

It served her purpose to allow everyone to assume that she had grown up in Hartford, Connecticut where she had worked for three years in one of the Big Six Accounting Firms after finishing college. The foolish part of the charade was that with each client Samantha took on, she usually became an officer of the company or a member of the Board of Directors; therefore, she had to file a lengthy biographical affidavit with the State's Department of Banking, Insurance & Securities. This form spelled out all the boring basics of her early Vermont years for any eyes that took the time to see. But when the simple statistics were laid out in black and white they seemed harmless.

As time passed and more and more of her history was erased from her memory, there were actually some days that she could almost make herself believe that she had come to this place via a different route. One that was more rational and predictable. One that some would call boring. One that she would have give anything for, if only it would fill the empty void within her heart.

Chapter 2

Growing up on Silver Pond, West Lexington, Vermont in the so-called Northeast Kingdom should have been idyllic. No one could ask for a more beautiful location. The calm, slightly rippling water is surrounded by tree covered mountains from every angle. The shoreline on the north side is broken up by the railroad tracks and a handful of year round homes; the backside has a few summer cottages, that can only be reached by the crudest of dirt roads, which is impassable eight months out of the year.

July and August are really hot and loud in the sun during the day, yet cool and quiet in the night, with the cricket and frog choruses trying to drown each other out in the pitch-blackness.

September and October bring the vibrant colors of Fall to the maple tree leaves. First the landscape is transformed and then the land itself, as they make their way from the branches to the ground. Sweatshirt weather means football games at Elkin Academy. One can make do by listening to them on the radio, but even better is attending in person; if a car and driver can be scraped up to make the sixteen-mile trek to town.

November is the beginning of the long and lonely winter, yet even the stark whiteness of the snow-laden hills and ice covered pond is broken up by familiar sights and sounds. The smoke from a wood burning stove and the laughter of children skating, skiing or snow shoeing, is never far away. Despite being able to see their own breath in the air, yet unable to feel any limbs, their energy never wanes. Tears form right in the ducts due to the wind-chill factor (always below zero) and then freeze on cheeks to form little icicles. The snowstorms come one after another and the drifts pile up until you can walk up a snowbank and onto your roof. Thanksgiving, Christmas and New Year's are always a blur of activities, as families gather together grandparents, aunts, uncles and cousins to celebrate all the blessings that the year has brought. And to pray for even more in the coming year.

Just when you think that winter will never end, the snow gives way to mud season. Slipping and sliding in watery, slimy muck that traps boots, tires and small animals will occupy everyone until the dryness returns in late June. And then the whole familiar cycle begins anew.

There is never a shortage of activities for the young or the old, although some are pleasant diversions while others are necessary evils. The snow that fascinates the babies and befriends the youngsters, becomes the sworn enemy of the elderly. People too old to be young, yet too young to be old, concentrate on simply making it through from one day to the next. Not so much living as existing.

Samantha knew that only a few of her classmates had decided to stay in the area and they were now struggling to raise families. The others felt the need to leave, in order to find a place where they could have some of what they were leaving behind, but also be able to pay for it. While her external excuse for going was the latter, internally, she couldn't wait to go where no one knew her and no one cared to. She had no intentions of ever dating, much less marrying and settling down with children of her own. No - she had no use for Silver Pond and what it had to offer.

When the colleges had descended upon her with full academic scholarships in hand, she didn't hesitate to take the money and run. For four years she kept her nose to the grindstone, never participating in a single social function. Her desire was to go on to law school, but when it was announced that she had made Valedictorian, the personal drive started to ebb. Job offers poured in and her resolve caved. The thought of three more years of study, while still not earning any money of her own, was too overwhelming. Finally, she made a decision. Just as accounting had won out in the Major lottery her sophomore year, this time a CPA firm took top honors. It was a salary that some chuckled at, but the little girl from Vermont couldn't believe how lucky she was.

Ironically her first year assignments were concentrated in the captive insurance field and she found herself traveling more and more to the Vermont management companies located within the 35 mile stretch between the largest city of Burlington in the northwestern part of the state and one of the smallest, the capitol of Montpelier, located in the exact center. The tangled knot of dread that had formed in her stomach at the thought of returning to the state disappeared the first time she flew over Lake Champlain. Landing at the Burlington International Airport was an incredibly liberating experience, like she had found something that she didn't even know she had lost. It helped that even when she was in Montpelier, the Northeast Kingdom was still an additional 35 miles up Route 2 - which in Vermont, is another world away.

She planned, plotted and saved for three years before she radically altered the path her life and career were on. The day came when she said goodbye to what few ties had been formed in Hartford and headed back to Vermont to build her own Management Company from scratch. Surely the rough and tumble shores of Lake Champlain would erase any memory of what had transpired on the deceivingly quiet shores of Silver Pond that lifetime ago, right?

It didn't happen overnight, but rather quickly in the overall scheme of things, she was operating the largest independent firm in the state. There was gossip within the community about who she had slept with in order to get the business going. Even more laughable (from her perspective), was the notion that a rich family member had given her the start up money. Since it would serve no useful purpose, she never attempted to correct any of these misconceptions. It was not important for others to know how hard she had worked for all that she had accomplished. It was enough to have actually done it.

Although she had no desire to tell the truth about her relatives, she was not interested in concocting fairy tales either. Clients and prospects found her reticence to share anything remotely personal slightly entertaining, along with her focus on their affairs 24 hours a day with 150% of her attention. It was more than the effort they expended themselves, but then again, that is what they paid her for. She made it her life's mission to know everything there was to know about the niche that she had literally fallen into.

Of course hiding under the pretense of being a Flatlander did have certain advantages. There were no silly conversations like: "Didn't you used to live on Pearl Street next to that huge house that didn't have its own driveway? You know, the one where those twin boys lived? Next to the beauty parlor? I'm sure you did."

"No, you're thinking of my mother's cousin."

There weren't any gasps of recognition while standing on the corner and having to overhear whispers of: "Oh my god, that's Catherine Atherton's granddaughter. You know, her daughter Miranda got pregnant by Alan Armstrong's boy - Bud - in high school. Alan's wife, you remember Sarah, made them get married and of course it was too much for the poor kids. The way I heard it, Bud was a no good drunk who ran off when the baby was only five. Miranda was never right in the head after that. One day she just snapped completely and up and killed herself! Yes, I tell you! Poor little Samantha is the one that found her mother, when she came in from playing one day. She was watching The Joker's Wild and just decided to kill herself. Can you imagine? No note, no nothing. Anyway, that's little Samantha. I'd bet my life on it. All grown up, she is. Oh, wait a minute, isn't that Billy Clark in front of the Ben Franklin Store? Did you know that his Aunt Agnes went to Santa's Village one hot summer day and..."

It was crazy how people grossly distorted the facts of such tragedies. Samantha's mother had been watching Jeopardy when she hung herself. If it had been any other show, Samantha would have been able to forgive her Mom, as well as herself. But she would never be able to forgive (or forget) Jeopardy.

Chapter 3

At five feet five inches tall with dirty blonde shoulder length hair and overall unremarkable features, Samantha was easily a woman who could walk through a room unnoticed. In fact, it was rare for her to receive a second look from anyone outside the office. It was only when she was draped in one of her expensive suits and made up to the max to unveil a new multimedia presentation on the hot topic of the hour that she was impossible to ignore. From the time her mother had left her on her own, she had worked very hard on honing the most valuable skill - the act of delivering the goods. The goods being whatever the grandparent, teacher, guardian, neighbor, client, etc. was looking for.

Gaining knowledge of a subject had always been a simplistic task for her; she was a living, breathing encyclopedia of facts and figures. School had served her well as an escape mechanism and she pursued knowledge relentlessly.

Business had seemed a logical course to follow, since there were so many options within that arena. Accounting had been a wonderful choice for her concentration and then Insurance was simply icing on the cake. If there was something she loved it was her work and she was grateful to have so much of her time tied up in the operation of her company.

Relationships were not a priority; she had not formed lasting friendships with anyone.

Samantha did not feel comfortable with her Grandmother (the woman who raised her) because she found it troubling that someone could remain virtually unchanged by their own child's death. Anger or bitterness would have been understandable, even preferred. Instead, the determination she exhibited trying to make her granddaughter's life more "normal" than was reasonable to expect was not admired.

Her grandfather had been a wise man that she respected deeply, and it had pained her to leave him behind in Vermont when she left. A secret hope was to one day move him into a grand estate wherever she ended up settling down after making her mark on the world. It had never occurred to her that he wouldn't have wanted to join her - but it didn't matter anyway. His old heart had given out long before Samantha had a chance to ask him.

She had not seen her Father's parents since that horrible day of the funeral. Both Grandmothers had screamed loud enough for the whole town to hear, when the Armstrongs had shown up at the town hall to pay their respects. Terrible, venomous things were spewed across the room. Truths, half-truths and untruths were aired for all to pretend they didn't notice.

Her father had always been a stranger to her, since his drinking, swearing and all around destructive behavior intruded on any fantasies she tried to maintain about having a real life with him. The dreams stopped completely that day he failed to return from the store when she was three. No one said a word to her, but she didn't need to hear it. She knew that he would never return to live in the cramped, unwelcome home of his in-laws.

Her mother had already settled for only going through the motions of getting out of bed in the morning, long before she finally ended her life. It was rare for her to do anything but watch television, although she actually talked during Jeopardy -or at least answered the questions. Sometimes she would even dress up for the Tournament of Champions.

When Samantha was fifteen, she found a high school yearbook in the attic. The contents shocked her. It was filled with information about her parents that didn't fit the couple she had known. Bud's formal senior portrait made her weak in the knees. He had been so handsome! As she turned the pages, she discovered that he had been captain of the Soccer, Basketball and Baseball teams. After years of listening to her Grandmother complain about "the bum" (when she thought little ears were out of range), she imagined that her father hadn't been lucky enough to attend school beyond the sixth grade. What had happened?

There were several hearts drawn around her mother's picture in the back section of the book. It was a candid that showed the Freshman Goddess in all her glory. She was surrounded by boys and girls alike, who were staring the same way Samantha did at the picture the first time she saw it. Her mother had to have been the most beautiful woman in the world. Had things been very different, she probably would have become Miss America or even a movie star. So she wondered again - What had happened to her parents who had shown such talent and promise????

It was no secret throughout the Kingdom what had transpired Bud Armstrong's last great year at the Academy. He was to head off to an Ivy

League college and become famous. That is, that was his father's plan before Bud had fallen head over heels in love with the very young Miranda. For the nine months during the school year they were inseparable. But the next nine months were the beginning of the end for them. They made the mistake of creating something that they couldn't handle and their parents wouldn't let them give up or destroy - a little girl they had named Samantha.

With no input from Miranda or Bud, it was decided that they would get married and move in with her parents on the Pond. Bud would take a job at the Paper Mill in Hodgeton with his Dad and by the time the baby was ready to start school, the couple would have saved enough for a house of their own.

Miranda was no longer the belle of the ball. She was removed from prying eyes and wagging tongues. For someone who had always thrived on the attention of others, the lack of social contact was devastating. She started to deteriorate physically and mentally. Bud felt trapped in a nightmare that he couldn't wake up from. First during the day when the other mill workers laughingly called him "College Boy" and then when he returned to Miranda and had to hold her as she sobbed uncontrollably throughout the night.

Nothing changed for either one of them when the baby was born. Their hellish existence continued unabated. Bud still went to the mill and hated it. Miranda was still inconsolable from dusk until dawn. Miranda's mother was the only one who enjoyed the baby. She was ecstatic to have her homely little granddaughter with colic all to herself.

The baptism brought the two families together for a brief moment of peace, before the arguments started about whose fault the disaster was and which life was in more ruinous shape. No one noticed the content grandmother rocking the bundle in the corner. She couldn't have been happier. Her daughter hadn't turned out the way she had planned, but God had been kind and given her another chance. She was confident that her age and experience lent the maturity she would need in the newly created position of Nanny. She had learned her lessons well... She wouldn't make the same mistakes with this child.

Chapter 4

One night Miranda stopped crying and the next evening Bud stopped coming home. Or he came home extremely drunk, very late at night and collapsed on the couch located on the pond side front porch. The only time he felt really free was when he was out there in the quiet darkness, either sweltering from the summer's unbearable heat or freezing from the winter's bitter cold.

Alcohol was also an escape for Miranda, but since she never left the house, she needed something more. Jeopardy became the one bright spot in her day. She felt like she was back in high school and if she played the game well and won the final round, she'd have a chance to erase that one small moment in her life when everything had changed.

* *

It had happened after Bud's final baseball game of the season. He was the happiest she had ever seen him and more than anything, she wanted that night to go on forever. All his friends were partying like tomorrow would never come, because they knew that it most certainly would. They were all headed their separate ways, so the mood of this moment couldn't last much longer. Miranda felt very special, being included in something so unique.

Bud told her that there was a surprise waiting at a friend's house beyond the football field. When the group was jockeying car positions, so everyone would have a seat, Bud vetoed riding and decided to walk instead.

"Go along without us... We'll meet you there in a few..." The night was clear and cool and since they would finally be alone, she had jumped at the idea.

By the time they had climbed the embankment from one field to the other, the alcohol was starting to wear off. Miranda was hit with the realization that after the short summer, Bud would be starting a new and exciting life without her. He would be far away from her (a mere girl), but extremely close to a lot of women his own age. Women who could offer so much more than her skin-deep beauty.

This is what was weighing heavily on her mind, when Bud grabbed her off the running track and pulled her down onto the wet grass with him. In a flash he had rolled her over and was now on top of her, kissing her mouth, nose and eyes with an urgency that she had never sensed before. His breath was burning her ear and neck and the bulge in his pants was pressing hard against her thigh. "Please God Miranda, you've got to help me relieve some of this pressure! I'm dying, baby. You know I love you. I'd do anything for you, honey, anything! Now it's your turn to prove you love me. Oh God how I love you!"

She didn't fight him, it didn't even occur to her to try. This was what she wanted to seal their union. Desperately she made love for the first and last time in her life. It was as incredible for her as it was for him, so when they lay spent in the dewy mist, shivering, there were no doubts that this was as good as it would ever get. The difference between them was that Bud thought it was only the end of one chapter in his life; Miranda knew that it was the end of everything for them both.

Each tortured day of her existence since she had found out that she was pregnant, she had replayed that scene over and over again in her head. The words of passion that had swayed her then, seemed so ridiculous now. In the revised version she liked to imagine, he always ended up disappointed and alone, after she laughed about his boyish lies. She hated herself slightly less than she hated him, but it didn't matter anymore. Nothing did.

She remembered very little between the romp on the athletic field and the moment she realized that Bud had left her. It was actually a tremendous relief to know that he would not be coming back. Her mother would have no reason to chant on incessantly about what a loser her big man had turned out to be. The punishment she suffered was what she had feared most that fateful night - being rejected; however, somehow it was ok for him to leave her now. Her body, complexion and hair had never recovered from the very difficult pregnancy. Even when she looked in the mirror, she didn't recognize the image that peered back. She didn't blame him for leaving her like this, but she wouldn't have been able to stand him leaving her back then. She wanted to run away like Bud had, but she didn't have the strength and she had no place to go. She had nothing.

One beautiful spring day Nanny asked Samantha to go to the post office with her and Grampy. That was not out of the ordinary, but when they didn't return home for lunch, she was confused. Usually her mother was not left alone for more than an hour at a time. Today was to be special she was told. Since Samantha was starting school in the fall, it was time for a shopping spree at Doral's. Samantha was giddy with excitement. She had never been inside the expensive shops that lined Main Street in Elkin, even though she had watched them many times with her Grandfather. His favorite pastime was to drive into town and sit in his parked truck for hours, just watching the people go by. He would tell Samantha stories about everyone they saw. Where they grew up, who their relatives were, what they did for a living, who they married, etc. Whenever he saw someone he didn't know, he would narrow his eyes and talk in a funny voice saying, "Now I vunder vhat he is up to?" Sometimes they would get out of the truck and follow the suspicious character, until they were satisfied that the Tourist or Flatlander posed no serious threat to anyone.

But this day was not like that, because Nanny was with them. It made her nervous, since it was getting dark, like it should be time for Jeopardy. She didn't want to miss the show; it was the only thing her Mother shared with her and pathetic as it was, it was better than nothing.

Finally they loaded up the pickup bed with bags of pants, skirts, shorts, tops, socks and underwear and headed up Route 2 toward home.

"Jesus Christ, what are they doing here... today of all days?" was the reaction from Nanny, when she saw Bud's parents' car at the foot of the steep driveway.

Samantha knew immediately that something was horribly wrong. She leapt from the cab before it had rolled to a complete stop and ran into the house to see what had triggered the terrible shrieking erupting from the living room. She noted the look of horror on her paternal grandmother's face and then slowly turned toward her mother's chair. It was empty, but above it she could see her mother's slippers seemingly dancing in midair. Then she took in the feet, legs, housecoat and finally her head cocked to one side, with the blue tongue hanging out the other. The eyes were open and straining to pop out of their sockets. Except for the odd expression created by this look, her mother appeared to be almost happy. She was finally free from her demons.

The music of final Jeopardy from the television broke through the madness and Samantha yelled "BE QUIET!!! Mom will kill me if she can't hear the last question!!!" In shock, everyone stopped whatever they were doing and watched the five-year-old who climbed up on the chair and held the dead woman's hand.

"Come on Mommy, this is an easy one. You know this one. Mommy? MOMMY? M-O-M-M-Y!!!!!" She remembered the deafening silence that followed when someone turned off the TV. She could still feel the sensation of being carried upstairs against her will. Everyone was crying, clasping their hands in prayer and rocking their bodies back and forth. Everyone except Nanny. Samantha watched in confusion through burning tears as she scattered all the papers from the dining room table, as well as the countertops which lined the walls from the kitchen to the bathroom, calling out something about a note that had to be there somewhere.

Samantha didn't need a note explaining why her Mother had committed suicide, she knew the reason. It was her fault. She had been out having fun (shopping of all things) and had forgotten about Jeopardy. Her Mom had felt deserted, so she deserted Samantha in return. The family tradition continued - history was just repeating itself. She was alone and destined to stay that way.

Chapter 5

By the time Samantha shook herself back to the present, clearing the cobwebs from the past, she realized it was already an hour and a half past the time she had planned to leave the office. Somehow the past kept worming its way back through that maze she had constructed to keep it contained. Why was it happening more and more these days?

Luckily tomorrow was Sunday, so she would have one more day of solitude in the office before the tide turned. As much as she enjoyed her weekends at work, she hated Monday. In desperation she tried to schedule a full morning of meetings "on the road" at the start of each workweek, so that her arrival into the office was timed after everyone had completed the necessary transmittal of weekend gossip to colleagues.

She knew it was much easier on all concerned if she could allow them those precious few hours of unsupervised, unstructured revelry. It was too irritating for her when she could hear workers bragging about how smashed they had gotten Friday night, or how little they could remember about the next day. If she needed to venture out to the copier or the fax machine, before the stories were exhausted, the thick silence that hung in the air managed to make even her uncomfortable.

The cruel form of initiation that her employees used on the new recruits also involved this painful exercise. The old hands would sit in their cubicles, their faces shielded and their mouths buried in their shoulders or fingers, as the poor slob who was starting his first job would come gliding in the very first day, march straight into her office and chirpily ask, "Did you have a good weekend, Ms. Armstrong?"

She knew that each time it happened her look of utter contempt got more and more frightening. Her response never varied, "Welcome to Champlain Risk Systems. If you'll see the Receptionist, she'll show you to your work area and get you started on the usual round of employment forms. I'll check in around 10 a.m. with your client assignments. Thank you."

It wasn't until lunch that the brave soul could relax, finally secure in the knowledge that he had only committed the same faux pas that all before him had. After being surrounded by solemn co-workers, eventually someone would break the tension with, "I'm sorry, I didn't hear the answer to your first query - How was Ms. Armstrong's weekend?" As the troupe collapsed in laughter, the new employee started to think that perhaps he'd survive long enough to collect that first paycheck after all.

Samantha didn't get any joy out of this charade, but she did think that it managed to knock everyone down a few notches, just as they were in the door getting their feet wet. She found this humiliation helpful, since cockiness in an employee was something she could not abide. It was a lot easier to let them know this up front, then to try and deal with an established pattern.

This particular upcoming Monday in March was not a day that Samantha had been looking forward to. Usually any day in this month was a delight, since CRS was coming off the high of meeting the February 28th annual statement regulatory filing deadline for all clients. But this day, she had fought like hell to avoid. She had a meeting scheduled first thing with one of her best clients, Mark Monahan, at his request. Although she thoroughly enjoyed the work she did on his account, this did not directly involve it. Samantha was being begged to give his son, Trevor, a position at CRS, when he graduated from Harvard in two months. All her reasoning against the move had fallen on deaf ears. Monahan had insisted on a face to face and he promised that Trevor would knock her socks off. She had met more than her fair share of Trevors over the years and the only thing that ever came close to being knocked off were their block heads.

Sunday had better be a day of rest... Monday was going to be a bitch...

Chapter 6

Leaving the building and locking up in the dark she made a mental note to have her assistant call maintenance about the outside lighting. This was the third time in two weeks that she was inching her way to the car feeling like Helen Keller. There wasn't much that scared her, but being in the pitch blackness of a deserted Burlington parking lot on a Saturday night was right up there. If it weren't for the elaborate sidewalk system intertwined with shrubs and benches, she could park right next to the door and be on her way within seconds of turning the key. Why did the other tenants not see what a nuisance this "park" was to their lives?

Finally she made it to the driver's side door after what seemed like an eternity, unlocked the car, threw her briefcase in the back, jumped in the front and quickly locked everything back up again. She smiled as she stepped on the gas and turned the key. Her grandfather would be proud to see that she had an American made car. A Real Vermonter to the end, he never bought anything that wasn't from the good ole U.S. of A. Of course he received a lot of "gifts" that were foreign made (mostly from his wife who bought them with his money!), but since it would have been rude and insulting to return them, he made do.

Samantha did miss him; when she finally got up enough courage to go visit her mother's grave, she would make a special effort to look up his as well. She had not returned to the

Kingdom for his funeral, which took place during her Senior Year of college. When the phone call came during finals week, she mechanically packed some clothes in her suitcase and took the shuttle to the bus station. An announcement came over the public address system that boarding would begin in five minutes, when suddenly she could hear her grandfather's voice very clearly. The words he spoke she had heard several times before, but at first she couldn't recall when.

"When I go, don't you dare cry for me and don't even think about wasting your time going to my funeral. Do something you love, or better yet, do something I loved. That will mean more to me than sitting around with people I wouldn't have in my house when I was livin'. Folks only cry at funerals because of guilt and regrets. I don't believe in guilt and I don't bother with regrets. You shouldn't either."

He had first said those words at his daughter's funeral, when Samantha asked him why he wasn't crying. She hadn't understood any of what he had said then, but it came up again when his brother died many years later. She had been in high school then, and as they wandered off from the rest of the mourners she had asked him question after question, trying to decipher his secret philosophy for overcoming pain.

"Blossum," he had said, "guilt is something that has been manufactured to make people feel better when they're doing something they ain't supposed to." Her puzzled expression had made him smirk and encouraged him to continue. "I'll give you an example. Some of the best sobbers up at the house right now are saying things like, 'I felt so guilty that I wasn't spending more time with Arthur near the end' and everyone is patting them on the back and handing them tissues while saying, 'Don't beat yourself up about it. We all did the best we could.' Well guess what? I don't buy it! A feeling of guilt should be a three-second wake up call. Something is not right and you need to make amends or make peace. Either A) I'm going to go see Arthur right now -or- B) I need to admit to myself that I'm a selfish, son of a bitch that doesn't want to be bothered going to a depressing, smelly nursing home to see a dying man. But that's not what happens anymore. We allow people to stay in that limbo state of guilt. 'I know I should go to see Arthur. I'm not going to, but at least I feel guilty about it, so I'm not a bad person.' Regrets work the same way. They're bullshit, Blossum. Always say what you mean and mean what you say. Don't have if-onlys in your life."

It was then that he had made her promise not to attend his funeral. In Hartford, ready to step on the bus that would take her back home to that very event, she took a taxi to Main Street instead. She found a bench on the sidewalk and sat there for hours in the rain watching the people go by. She made up stories about who they were and what they did for a living. Every once in a while she narrowed her eyes and started to talk in a funny voice, "Now I vunder vhat she is up to?", but she stopped short of following anyone. She felt her grandfather's presence and knew he was satisfied (as long as the rain masked the view of her tears from his perch in heaven).

Once again Samantha had to shake herself loose from her thoughts. This time it was at a stoplight that had been green for quite some time. Luckily the kind stranger in the car behind was sending her a medley of sounds and gestures that were quite helpful in getting the trip home back on track... What was wrong with her today?

Chapter 7

It was one of those nights when she couldn't recall driving home. All of a sudden she would "wake up" to realize that she was pulling into her driveway and yet she didn't even remember where she had come from. She had never been in an accident, but a feeling that her luck was just about to run out was intensifying.

The momentary concern was erased the minute she caught sight of her house. She loved the look of her "castle" from all angles - the road, the water, hell... even the sky. It wasn't as large as some of her peers', but it was comfortable and on Lake Champlain, which were the two priorities the real estate agent was given when the hunt began for the perfect home for a successful, single (with intentions to stay that way) executive. The cottage was certainly adequate for her needs (only shelter these days) and had proved quite the showplace for her personal assistant. While Samantha would entertain clients on a few rare occasions, Jeannie had parties almost every weekday and on weekends whenever her employer was not around.

Samantha had no use for Jeannie's crowd, but as long as they left the house the way they found it, she could put up with the nonsense. It wasn't anything that was spoken of. Jeannie knew that Samantha didn't like it, but would tolerate it to a certain extent; Samantha knew that Jeannie would never go too far as to take advantage of her or her generosity. If there was ever a second when Jeannie couldn't perform her duties because of a hangover, that would be the end of their partnership. Neither could live with that. They had a wonderful understanding, but like everything else in Samantha's life, how they met was quite an odd tale.

On her way back from a client board meeting in Colorado, Samantha got stranded at O'Hare. It was extremely aggravating, because she had planned her flights tight from the outset. She was due back to Burlington for another meeting in six hours and since she had left the agenda materials for that account back on her desk, she couldn't even brush up on the topics while she waited.

There was only so much pacing she could do within the terminal, as the flight could have been called at any minute. No matter how hard she tried, it was too difficult to concentrate on a newspaper or magazine. Where ever she sat in the gate area, all she could hear was the sobbing of a beautiful young girl in the far corner. It appeared that she would straighten herself up, blow her nose, dry her tears, give herself some words of encouragement, only to collapse in heart wrenching cries of grief again. Samantha had unwillingly witnessed this scene not less than five times in slightly under ten minutes. Although it was getting old, she couldn't help stealing glances in her direction and wondering what the story was behind this performance. (Shades of her Grandfather's influence, no doubt!)

She began to wonder what terrible tragedy had struck this poor creature. Well, she didn't exactly look poor. Samantha had no eye for fashion (as in what colors/styles etc.

look good together or on her), but she certainly knew when someone else was wearing very expensive clothing. More than once she had wanted to die of embarrassment when she was traveling and had people say things like, "Oh my, did the airline lose your luggage - again? Did *they* pick out that outfit, or did you?" Clients never said anything or reacted negatively, it was always the wives who got several tee-hees out of her ensembles.

While her Grandfather's voice was urging her to try and help the stranger in need, Samantha's own inner voice was singing a personal favorite: Curiosity killed the cat! There - the boarding announcement finally came over the loudspeaker. She wasn't home free yet, but she was starting to relax. It was a big plane and what were the odds that she would be seated anywhere near that great geyser of tears?

The line to the podium where the ticket agent stood profusely apologizing to all who passed through the ropes on the way to the plane was quite long. Samantha was not one to rush to get to her seat, especially this day, since her client had thoughtfully paid for a first class ticket. There was no point in dashing madly into the angry mob only to stand pushing and being pushed for 15 minutes - the end results were the same.

When she finally ventured out of her chair and got in line behind the disgusted family of five from Italy, she almost felt like her old, normal self again. "Excuse me," said the quiet voice behind her. Unless she was blessed by the appearance of two women who were emotional wrecks today, it had to be the one she had been spying on earlier. Maybe she wasn't talking to her. If she just kept staring straight ahead, appearing to be in some sort of drug induced stupor, maybe she would go away. No such luck.

"Excuse me, Ma'am?" and this time Samantha felt pressure on her right elbow and was turned to face the inquisitor. She was even lovelier up close, despite the smudged mascara and runny nose. Samantha decided she hated her and was determined to answer any query with incorrect and down right misleading information.

"Yes?" she whispered looking around suspiciously for the hidden camera or the woman's thieving accomplice. "Can I help you with something?" she couldn't believe her own ears, when the words she had vowed not to say rolled off her tongue.

"Is this plane going to Vermont?"

Oh no, God is stingy when he is handing out that rare combination of good looks and a brain, isn't he? "Yes, Burlington." Of course the clarifier of a city was unnecessary, since if a plane was going to Vermont, it was going to Burlington... but hey, maybe Samantha hadn't heard correctly, maybe she had said Virginia or something. Never can be too careful when answering questions - it's always a good practice to be clear.

"Is this a real ticket that will get me there?" she asked pathetically, as she held out an envelope for Samantha to verify.

"I believe so... it looks just like mine. See?" Indeed, the ticket looked just like hers - was it Friday, the 13th or something? Who was this loser?

"Well to be honest, I've never flown before. My... My... My boyfrie... My... OHHHHHH" The flood gates opened up again and somehow

Samantha sensed that soon she would know more than she ever wanted to know about another human being's woes.

As luck would have it, not only were the two traveling mates, but they were the only passengers in first class as well. By the time the pilot turned off the fasten seat belt sign, Samantha had heard the whole twisted tale of Jeannie's ill fated affair with a married man, who had promised her the sun and the moon, but had only delivered on two first class plane tickets for a romantic getaway. He had realized too late that he couldn't leave his precious wife after all. It seemed that they shared too much - mostly her money!

Samantha alternated between the vision of running from the plane, hopping in a taxi, leaving her luggage abandoned on the carousel, never to return to the airport for fear of encountering this poor soul again - to - simply wanting to put her coat and arm around the waif, while asking which of her three guest bedrooms she would like for her very own, to stay as long as she liked, rent free of course.

Reality was a compromise of helping her cash in the weasel's unused ticket at the customer service counter in Burlington and directing her to a reduced rate motel located conveniently next to Samantha's office. They made plans to meet at The Bagel Hole for breakfast the following morning, after a sworn oath was administered that things would look a hell of a lot better by the light of day. Jeannie had no doubts that Samantha was a woman of her word and could make things happen; Samantha knew that Jeannie would be her responsibility from that night forward and amazingly accepted the fact without question or concern.

By the end of the week, Jeannie's money was gone, but she had hammered out a deal with her savior. In exchange for room, board and a small salary, she would provide Samantha with coiffure guidance (hair care), fashion assistance (clothing purchases) and home maintenance services (house cleaning). It didn't concern Jeannie that she knew nothing about Samantha, other than the obvious things her outward appearance screamed, i.e. that she desperately needed a new hairdo and a suit that was designed after 1950!

Samantha was confident that she was getting the most out of the arrangement that was intended to be temporary (currently going on two years). She picked up the things that her business persona was sorely lacking and it didn't cost her any time or effort (just money, which she could spare). But most of all, she could sometimes pretend that Jeannie was more than her employee. On days that she felt sorry for herself, when she would wake up in a cold sweat because she was old and alone, she could feel better by almost making herself believe that she finally had something that she had never had before - a friend.

Chapter 8

All these thoughts came crashing down around Samantha the minute she came into the mudroom from the garage. There were coats, shoes, socks & various other unidentifiable items scattered on the floor throughout this section of the house. Sounds of hysterical laughter carried from the living room with loud shushing sounds that seemed to only intensify the giggling.

She could hear Jeannie's loud, drunken pleas of "You guys, p-l-e-a-s-e... she's going to be soooooo pissed at me!" and more laughter. Her heart sank. Something that she would have bet a million dollars against happening not five minutes earlier was happening. Tears stung her eyes as she heard herself mutter a most inappropriate response to the situation, "Shoot." The Real Vermonter came out of her at the oddest times!

One look in the mirror assured her that the wet eyes were not betraying her true feelings, so she headed around the corner to greet the partiers. Whatever mental preparations she thought had been made, were forgotten as the smoke and smell of the marijuana overwhelmed her. The sight of potato chip bags and crumbs all over her furniture and chunks of brownies ground into her carpeting stirred an anger deep inside her. The silence of the "guests", along with their strained expressions from holding their breath for fear of bursting into fits of laughter, proved to be too much.

"GET OUT OF MY HOUSE!" she screamed at the top of her lungs, while running around the room slapping the idiots who didn't seem to comprehend that they were dealing with a woman possessed. If anything, the snickering compounded, as each person who was reached would cower and say something like, "Oooo, the big bad boss lady is home. I'm soooo scared!"

Jeannie sat on the floor rocking back and forth like she were about to urinate - unsure if she too was supposed to heed the order and leave or if Samantha had something else in mind for her. She didn't know which was the lesser of the two evils, so she waited to hear what her employer was going to opt for.

Samantha clawed at the curtains and ripped the shade right off the roller trying to find the way to open the window. After several minutes of straining to get the screen exposed, she realized that the lock was thrown on the top of the sill. She hit that a few times for good measure, yelled some obscenities and then finally was able to get the rush of cool air. Her hand was throbbing, had it been broken? She could feel the breeze pulling at her damp shirt. How did she get so wet? Was it raining outside? Did she get that sweaty simply running from one end of the house to the other? Her fight with the window?

Her head ached and her mind was racing. What was she going to do? She couldn't live without Jeannie... she did everything... the cooking, cleaning, shopping... her hair! My God, she put her hair up every morning! She set her clothes out every night - she packed for her business trips. She knew that Jeannie had an elaborate system of index cards that told what accessories had been worn when, with what clients, in order to save her the embarrassment of constantly greeting the same client with the same outfit. Samantha had no time for such nonsense, but she knew it was important to her image.

Of course Jeannie knew this too. She knew that she had made herself indispensable. What a fool Samantha had been. Oh how they must have been laughing behind her back. In her own house, sitting around talking about what a moron she was. The pictures that were forming in her mind were unbearable. She wanted to collapse into tears and ask Jeannie, "Why? How could you do this to me?", but she didn't want to give her the satisfaction. Instead she wanted to hurt her as much as she had been hurt by this betrayal. What a big mistake Jeannie had made. Oh how she would pay for it.

"Samantha I am so sorry. Please let me explain..." Finally the gravity of the situation sunk in and Jeannie jumped to her feet trying to calm Samantha down. It served no purpose now, but she was still running around the room. Jeannie put her hand gently on her arm, prepared to give her a hug, but Samantha roughly threw her aside.

"Don't you touch me! I want you out of my house - NOW!"

"Samantha, you don't mean that. Listen to me, you don't understand. They've been torturing me for months. I couldn't take it anymore!"

"What the Hell are you talking about?"

"Day after day, they'd pepper me with: 'Why do you put up with her? She treats you like a slave. What happens when she's bored with you? Where does that leave you? None of this is yours - it's all hers - she likes letting you see that she has it all and it can be taken away from you with the snap of her fingers. What does she want from you? Does she love you? Are you her girlfriend? What kind of future do you have?' It was relentless. Tell me you understand what I've been going through, please!"

"I still have no idea what you are talking about!"

"My friends - they kept telling me that I don't really have a future. I mean this job has been right up my alley, because I don't have any skills, but what am I going to do with the rest of my life?"

"You stupid bitch! Do you even have a brain in that big fat head of hairspray??? I was taking care of you and I would have done that forever! Look around you. Was your life so hard? What, was the pool not big enough for you? Your room too small? Your salary not enough for your drug habit? Your clothes allowance too measly for your high society, high school drop out freaks? Your friends - Your friends - get a fucking clue and get some new friends! Don't betray me! Don't throw your life away, because of some losers you met at a bar!"

"I know, I know. You're right. I'm sorry. Oh God, Samantha, you're right. I know. Thank you. Thanks for understanding. You're right. Don't worry, it won't happen again."

"You're damn right it won't. We're through. You're through. It's over - here - take this & get out..."

Samantha ran into the den and Jeannie could hear drawers opening and closing with great force. Jeannie sank onto the couch and held her head in her hands as the tears began to spout. She heard a noise and looked up just as Samantha came flying back into the room and threw a folder at her. Papers and envelopes scattered all over the room. She couldn't tell what all the items were, but there were official looking documents with seals on them and other statements with lots of numbers. Bank statements? Some sort of certificates?

"Samantha, what are you doing? Please, give me another chance. I said I was sorry."

"Sorry doesn't cut it Jeannie. I'm through with you. I don't give second chances. I never want to see you again. You are the most pathetic creature I have ever laid eyes on. Take your things and get out! Good luck finding some other poor sucker to take you in. Hey, what am I saying? I have no doubts that you will be successful within the hour!"

"What's all this?" Jeannie managed to ask, as she started to mechanically pick up the mess, while the tears continued to roll down her cheeks.

"It's the retirement plan I started for you a year ago, when I thought our arrangement had become permanent. You've got quite a little stock and bond portfolio going there, so do me a favor and don't let one of your new asshole friends get a hold of it. I would say that right now you are in the exact position that they were warning you about. The funny thing is, if it weren't for them, you wouldn't be in it. Ironic, isn't it?"

"Samantha, you don't mean any of this. Do you? Come on, you're overreacting!"

"Sorry Jeannie - my privilege. Now get out."

"You know what, Samantha? They were right. You are the most selfish, irritating, snobby, know it all that ever lived. What you need is a good fuck. I'm outta here, so it won't be from me, but you really do need to get a life."

"Oh I see the connection. I fire you for trashing my house, yet none of this would have happened if I would get a life! Well I have a life, Jeannie. You're the one that doesn't. And you never will. You will always need some poor sap that will feel sorry for you and take care of you. At least I'm through being the sap. Thanks for the learning experience. I'll remember this one for a long, long time. And for the record, the last thing I need (or want) is a sex life with you or anyone else. You really are something else - Good riddance!"

The argument had kept her mind working and the blood flowing through her body, but the minute the door slammed signaling that Jeannie was really gone, Samantha couldn't keep her composure any longer. She fell onto the nearest chair (potato chip crumbs and all) and let the total betrayal sink in to her bones.

It was like a knife in her heart to hear how Jeannie had let strangers convince her that their relationship was something other than what it was. What had she said, "Are you her girlfriend?" Is that what people thought? Samantha had never even considered the possibility that people would think she was a lesbian. She began to laugh. How funny it really was. It's not like she wasn't sometimes attracted to men - she often was; however, most of the men she came into contact with were either clients or business associates and she would never consider going out with someone like that. Of course no one had ever asked her before, so she never really had to think about it. She was just an old maid virgin who couldn't imagine that sex could be anything near what it was cracked up to be.

How much better than a rewarding career could it be? But what if her career wasn't as all-fulfilling as she had always made herself believe? Why could she not stop the onslaught of memories that kept flooding her subconscious - her mother and father, the grandparents that raised her, the college life that had flown by so quickly and had been so completely barren of social events, friends, fun?

Maybe she could use "a good fuck", as Jeannie had so eloquently put it. "Is Mark Monahan still married?" she wondered as she drifted off to sleep in the early hours of Sunday. For the first time in a long time, something personal was added to her list of things to do. She'd have to do some research on this one, but she was going to try. Try and get a life...

Chapter 9

Why was her head killing her? Had she been assaulted while leaving the office? Oh, no, now she remembered the drive home. Something had happened once she arrived. That's right, Jeannie. Jeannie had betrayed her. She had been laughing at her behind her back for two years. That's why her head hurt. She had screamed until the veins came close to bursting from her temples. She had never shown so much emotion.

What was that smell? Yes, all the details were back now. The party had been in full swing when she had broken up the revelry.

What had she done? Jeannie was gone. Her only friend had begged for forgiveness and she had been shown the door. No second chances. That was a rule and damn it, rules were made to be enforced! Why did everyone else insist on breaking the rules? Why couldn't anyone follow the Goddamn rules?

Chapter 10

She didn't go into the office on Sunday. In fact, she didn't move off the couch until it was almost noon. It had been a long time since she had done absolutely nothing for hours upon end.

Sometimes when she was a little girl, she would go down to the pond, climb over some rocks that lined the shore and settle on a very large, flat one that was out in the water a way. Whether it was a beautiful sunny day, or a cool rainy one, it didn't matter. She would just sit and take in the sights, sounds and smell of Silver Pond. Her mind would be emptied; it would be an exercise of the senses only.

She longed for that rock and that water now. For a brief moment she toyed with the idea of jumping in the car and driving to West Lexington, but then the fantasy that had been building was replaced with a different image. Had it been possible to get to the rock without encountering her Grandmother, she would have done it. But that wasn't reality. Nanny wouldn't be venturing too far from the house these days and even if Samantha parked at the beach and walked back up the railroad tracks, someone would be bound to see her. It wouldn't be long before her solitude was cut short and she wasn't prepared to visit with anyone, least of all her Grandmother.

How funny that the fear gnawing at her insides was the fear of being alone forever. And yet at the same time, she couldn't bear the thought of being with anyone else on earth right now.

She finally stood up and stretched - her muscles crying out in agony. It seemed like she had been immobile for months. She took a long, leisurely shower. The water was too hot, but she didn't try to adjust the temperature, she simply accepted the pain as a form of punishment.

In the bedroom, she surveyed her naked body in the full-length mirror as if seeing it for the first time. Samantha was not a beautiful woman. She could see and admit that; however, she was by no means ugly. What did it mean that no one had ever asked her out on a date? It was understandable given her demeanor. Didn't her attitude just shriek, "I am not interested in anything but work!"?

There was a drawer in her dresser that held sweaters and sweat pants that still had the tags from the stores on them. She chose an oversized gray sweatshirt and a pair of flowered leggings, then used her teeth to cut through the plastic ties. Dropping the endless assortment of advertising flyers, size listings and washing instructions into the trash, she prayed silently that the first outfit in two years that she had picked out herself didn't look too ridiculous.

She made her way back through the house, ignoring the mess that she had forgotten would still be there. In the mudroom closet she found a pair of sneakers that must be hers, they were too sparkling white to be Jeannie's. They felt odd on her feet - maybe it was the sensation of not wearing socks, but more likely it was the feeling of something other than the heels she had worn since high school.

Underneath the back of the house she found what she was looking for. It was a canoe that didn't appear to be seaworthy, but Samantha didn't care. If it turned out to be her time to leave this world, so be it. She could think of worse ways than drowning.

It was time to laugh at the irony in her life again. She had required a house on the Lake, but not once had she ever ventured into the water since moving back to Vermont. Amazingly both she and the canoe arrived down at the water in one piece and she started to glide out into Lake Champlain.

Before long she was unbearably hot, with sweat dripping down her face and stinging her eyes. The clothes she had picked out didn't seem so practical anymore.

She used the paddle to not only move out into the water, but also to reach over the side and splash some refreshment into the canoe and over her sweltering body. She quickly realized what a mistake that had been. Her temperature shifted dramatically. As much as she wanted to turn around and go home, she couldn't. Not until every ounce of her strength was gone would she allow herself to stop. The canoe drifted for awhile and then when the cold in her limbs and the ache in her back was no longer bearable, she finally turned to make her way back to the warm, inviting house on the shore.

Another hot shower and then she gathered her courage to face the kitchen. It was easy to find the coffee maker and quite clear how the appliance worked; however, she still had to unearth the filters and find where Jeannie had hidden the coffee beans. The first place to look had seemed logical - the canister marked "Coffee". But that was full of matchbooks from area bars. These must be collectors' items, now that smoking was banned in most places within the state.

"Thanks again, Jeannie," she whispered, as she made a mental note to call an acquaintance of hers who ran a local bed and breakfast. He'd love to get his hands on these. Often her clients would call for unique overnight accommodation suggestions (since they were all from out of state), so Samantha had a long list of potential service providers who checked in with her frequently and constantly lavished enticing gifts on her. It wasn't really such a bad life, was it?

The canister listing "Tea" as the contents checked out. After briefly flirting with the idea of having a cup of the weak liquid that her Grandmother used to force down her throat when she was ill, Samantha moved on to the two larger containers on the shelf above her head.

She hadn't been able to stomach anything but strong coffee first thing in the morning (or in this case, late in the afternoon), since her early CPA days. If she didn't find the beans soon, she would be in full-blown caffeine withdrawal. She might have to go out to buy a cup elsewhere and how sad a commentary on her life would that be?

"Sugar" turned out to be assorted candles of various colors and sizes. "Flour" was nothing but air. After opening and closing several cabinets with no better luck, Samantha went in to change her clothes for the third time today.

Every move she made this Sunday involved a decision she was not used to making. Did Jeannie really handle all the trivial day to day items that she had long forgotten how to do herself? Perhaps she needed to reconsider the one mistake and you're out of here policy, because the chance of surviving until Monday was looking rather dismal.

She managed to pick out another outfit from Hell and put a head band in her hair before climbing into her car and heading to The Bagel Hole for that medicinal cup of Java. She needed to eliminate the awful pounding in her skull.

She ordered a large cup of the Flavor of the Day and sat in a dark, back corner savoring the burn that started with her lips, went on to the tongue, and finished well down her throat.

Of course going to The Bagel Hole was a conscious, painful choice-just another reminder of Jeannie, since that was where their "arrangement" had been born. It began to sink in that perhaps the losers who were feeding Jeannie's fear of abandonment, weren't exactly way off the mark in terms of who was getting the short end of the stick here.

If only she could close her eyes and make things go back to the way they were before. If only she could turn back time and stay later at the office last night. Jeannie hadn't meant for the party to go so long. Had she? She had intended to have everything cleaned up before Samantha came home, right?

Apparently not, since Samantha had actually been quite late (thanks to her day dreaming escapades). Maybe Jeannie had wanted to get caught. Maybe she had wanted out and couldn't find another way to be set free. Free. What did that mean, anyway? If anything, Samantha was free - so why, then, did she feel so trapped?

She left half of the coffee on the table still steaming and got back in her car.

Without planning to, she drove to the Ferry and ended up crossing the Lake to New York. She drove on roads without knowing where she was or how or when she was going to get back home. But at precisely the right time she was back at the Ferry Landing and caught the last Boat back across Champlain.

Jeannie was not there waiting for her, nor had she visited the house in Samantha's absence. The place was still a mess, but there was nothing to be done tonight. Samantha pulled her clothes off with the last ounce of strength she could muster - letting them fall in a trail from the bedroom door to the mattress, where she collapsed, on her still made bed. How much longer could this torturous existence go on?

Chapter 11

The Jeopardy music was playing. She was back at her Grandparents' house and she was holding someone's hand. Without opening her eyes, she knew it was her Mother who was beside her. She was hanging just like the day they found her, except this time, Samantha was hanging also. Her throat was closed and she couldn't breathe. Was she dead?

Wait. What was that ringing? Was there a telephone on Jeopardy?

Samantha jumped up with a start to find herself in her bedroom, alone - exactly where she had fallen the night before. The ringing was persistent and finally broke through the dreamy fog. It was her telephone, on the nightstand. As she mechanically reached for it, her heart leapt in her chest as she took in the sunlight streaming through the curtains and the bedside clock that flashed the time of 9:15am MONDAY MORNING!

"To quote Mr. Monahan exactly," sobbed Samantha's assistant through the phone lines, "Where the frig is she?"

Despite feeling that her life had just ended (between the nightmare about her Mother and the fact that she had just upset her most important client), Samantha laughed. "Now Michaela, did he really say frig?"

She could picture the confused expression that had to be at the other end of the phone and half expected to hear, "I'm sorry, I've got the wrong number" followed by a click. Instead she heard a giggle and a whispered,

"No, he didn't. But he did say you have 15 minutes to get in here and kiss his ass before he fires yours!"

"Tell him I'll be there in 10 all puckered up and ready to go!" She didn't bother hanging up, she just threw the phone in the general direction of the cradle, as she jumped off the end of the bed and grabbed whatever clothes her hands found as she pulled handles that hopefully had appropriate work fare. With her taste, what difference did it make?

Mark Monahan. Hmmmm. I wonder if he's still married...

Chapter 12

The confidence she felt driving like a maniac to what she was positive was a firing, was something she had never experienced before. She had personally terminated so many people, she didn't even consider keeping track; however, she had never lost a job (or an account) herself, since she had started working.

There was no need to bother practicing a speech that would beg for forgiveness or attempt to offer some plausible explanation for her inappropriate behavior or appearance this morning. She had no intention of trying to change Monahan's mind. She had been dreading this meeting for a very long time, because she knew that against her better judgment, she would have gone along with his request. Now that scenario had been replaced with something completely new and unexpected. What was it going to be like? How furious was he going to be? What types of things would he scream at her? A thrill of excitement shot through her, revitalizing her body, as she imagined all sorts of twists and turns that could come from this experience.

She spent the wild ride to the office with the window down taking large gulps of fresh, cold Vermont air. Breathing, deeply, for the first time in a long time.

Should she just laugh when Mark reacted to her attire or would it be better to take this act to the edge and really pour on the craziness? Maybe she could get all her employees so upset that they would walk out as well - hell, run out - to save their sanity!

Everything she had built was about to come crashing down around her and she didn't care. Was she still dreaming? Or already insane?

Her fellow commuters were voting for the latter as they watched her weave through traffic talking to herself, laughing all the way. She called to them, wishing them well as they cut her off (or she they). Some received waves or were blown kisses - in return she accepted a lot of obscene gestures or simple headshakes.

It took exactly eight minutes for her to get to the building after receiving the call. In another two minutes she would be greeting Mark. Add another two minutes to that and she might be back on the road headed to God knows where. In any event, she would truly be a free woman! A date with Monahan was certainly out of the realm of possibilities now, but she'd grab her Rolodex on the way out, so she could make some calls and set up something on that front.

She took the stairs two at a time, arriving on the 4th Floor a lot faster than the old elevator would have brought her up. Unfortunately she missed out on the one advantage that taking the time to ride allows - being able to breathe when entering the office. She half ran, half stumbled into the reception area and was greeted by a very solemn group of individuals.

"Hey guys! How was everyone's weekend?" she gasped.

When the silence and stares were sustained, she continued. "Is Mr. Monahan in my office, Michaela?"

"W-h-a-t?" Michaela asked, while desperately trying to comprehend the sight in front of her. She turned slowly to her co-workers with her palms stretched upward and outward, as if they could help make sense out of this circus.

"Oh, there you are buddy," Samantha said as the inner sanctum's door was yanked open and Mark bounded out toward them. He had the same incredulous expression on his face. "Sorry I'm late. Thanks for being a pal and waiting for me." Standing on her tiptoes, she pecked him on the cheek and then walked briskly past him.

"What the HELL has happened to you?" he shouted, as he lunged for her elbow and missed. He glanced around the room and confirmed that everyone was in the same boat as he.

"Mark? Are you coming?" It was Samantha calling from inside the office. He threw his hands up in the air and followed her in. She indicated a chair at her conference table and then gently closed the door behind them, after leaning out and giving her stunned staff a thumbs up signal.

"Hi, how are you doing?" she nodded to the young man sitting at her desk. It had to be the wonder boy she was supposed to be interviewing for a job. How appropriate that he was already seated in her chair. She certainly wouldn't need it for the rest of the day, after his father raked her over the coals.

"Trevor, go across the street and get me a cup of coffee. I need to speak with Ms. Armstrong alone."

Trevor smiled and put his feet up on her desk. "Oh I don't think so, Pop. She can have her secretary get you some... I'm not going anywhere!"

Apparently his father had other ideas. "I said across the street."

"But there's a machine right out near the copier. I can..." He was cut off with a look and a "I said NOW!"

"OH. Sure, of course, Pop. Sorry. Right away." Samantha gave him a cutesy smile to replace the one that he had lost and then thankfully he was gone.

She had no problem with what was about to happen; in fact she was having a lot of fun with it. But to have it witnessed by a spoiled, rich kid who was born with more than she could ever dream of having, would put a damper on everything.

Mark went behind her desk and sat down where Trevor had been, but didn't get as comfortable. His feet remained planted firmly on the floor. He gestured to a straight back chair and started to chuckle and smile in the same way that he had observed Samantha doing since her astonishing arrival.

"Samantha. Sammy. Sam. You've got to help me out here. What has come over you? Are you drunk, honey?"

"No, Marky Mark, I've not been drinking. Just had a close encounter with a canoe last night. Overslept this morning. Sorry 'bout that, chief!" They both were giggling now and Samantha wondered exactly how long this axe falling thing was going to take.

Monahan shook his head and said, "A canoe? In this weather? You crazy Vermonter, you... I LOVE IT! It's about time you did something besides work."

Samantha stopped laughing. Something was going wrong. Things had taken a turn, but not in the way she expected. He didn't seem sarcastic anymore. He seemed to be over his anger and about to get down to business. What was wrong with him? Did she have to draw attention to how ridiculous she looked? When Trevor got back should she run through a quick highlight film of what a pathetic example of lack of professionalism she had just been to his precious little boy?

"Listen, I don't have much time. This has been a hoot, I'll give you that, but as you know, I've got to catch a plane. Trev graduates next month. I know the little wise ass needs a strong guiding hand to show him the ropes, but I can't have him at Home Office. I'd be too soft on him and everyone else would eat him for Breakfast, Lunch and Dinner. I know I've spoiled him rotten, but he's a good kid. Please Samantha, you're the only one I trust to do this. Although you did have me going just now! Come on, will you do it?" Monahan winked and Samantha pinched her arm, willing herself to wake up from this nightmare.

"Mark – I'll make a wager with you. If that kid can make it through a serious interview with me, standing on his own two feet as Joe Smith, not Trevor Monahan, Mark Monahan's son looking for special favors, he's got a job. But I'm telling you right now that's not going to happen. I've seen his kind a million times before and they just can't cut it. They don't have to and frankly they don't want to!"

"Samantha, you do it any way you want. He either makes the cut or he doesn't, you call it."

"Ok. Here he comes now. Give me thirty seconds and then send him in. You'll have to wait out there, I want to talk to him alone."

"Deal. Thanks, honey." Monahan took the coffee from his son and handed it to Michaela with a request for her to go dump it. He put his arm around Trevor's shoulders and gave him a twenty five-second pep talk. Unknown to either of them, Samantha was digging in her desk drawer for her long forgotten microcassette recorder. She turned it on and plopped it into her pocket, just as the two reentered the office.

"Here we are, back on track. Trevor, this is my good friend, Samantha Armstrong. Samantha, my son, Trev-uh, Joe Smith." He added that last part with a wink and a smile, which broadened when he saw the confused look on his son's face. He closed the door and went to talk with Michaela, who was still flustered.

As if on cue, the six incoming phone lines all lit up at once and everyone returned to their desks. Printers, copiers and fax machines were quickly humming away as if none of this had ever happened.

Back in Samantha's office, the two adversaries were smirking at one another, as both felt they were sitting in the driver's seat. "So Trevor, why should I hire you?"

"Well let me see... could it be because my father is as rich as the Queen of England, as powerful as God and he... oh, I don't know... fucking told you to?"

"Uh, huh. I see. Interesting. Please have a seat. No, I believe I will sit at my desk, you can have this chair." She was careful to keep the smile plastered on her face as she glanced out the window and caught Mark's eye. He nodded and smiled, confident that things were going as swimmingly as he had promised her.

"I believe the first change I'll make is that this will become MY office. I really like the view of the Lake, but then again, how much will I really be here working, right babe?"

This couldn't have been going better. She had pegged him correctly from the instant she had heard about him, never mind met him. "You know, Trev, should I decide to hire you... and I've got to be honest here... it's not really looking that good right now... you would have a cubicle out with the rest of the peons. Also, please note that if you ever refer to me as anything other than Ms. Armstrong again, I'll have to kick your testicles up into your eyeball area."

"Look, babe. I'VE got to be honest here. We both know that you're history. I don't know what kind of relationship you've had with Moses out there, but you are so fired it's not even funny. This is my little kingdom now. You'll have to find yourself another fucking gig. And here's some advice. Number one, look in a goddamn mirror before you leave the house - Jesus! Number two, don't be screwing the senile guy who's as old as dirt, when you could be tasting the sweet, young guy, who's really in charge and has all the power anyway!"

"Hmmmmm. I see. Well, Mr. Monahan, I guess we are just playing games here, aren't we? Except for a few minor details. Here's where I can offer you some advice. Granted, it's from a Babe, from the old school, on my way out, but here goes. Number one, before you go shooting your stupid mouth off - get a fucking clue! Your father owns a lot, but not my company ass hole! He hired me to manage his captive insurance company and he's probably going to fire me, but he's only one of my seventy clients. Number two, you might want to actually read up on his holdings-you know, do some research? I have a feeling you're headed to home office now, BABE! Mark's a brilliant, wonderful man, who knows more about business than you ever will my friend. If you decide right now to completely change your attitude, you just might manage to make something of yourself. But somehow, I doubt you're going to do that."

She barely heard the soft knock on the door before she looked up and saw that it was Michaela. Disgustedly she asked why they were being disturbed.

"I'm sorry. There's a Bill Morgan on line three who insists on speaking with you. He won't say what it's about, just that he's positive you want to take his call."

All the enjoyment derived from drinking in the stunned look on Trevor's face was gone in a second. Samantha had a sick feeling deep in her stomach and could feel the bile rising in her throat, even though it wasn't registering who the caller was.

"Mark?" she called out. "Can you come in here, please?" Briefly she regained a triumphant feeling by extracting the recorder from her pocket and throwing it past Trevor to Mark, who snapped it up like an expert receiver.

"I'm sorry to do this, but I think you and your son need to go in Peg's office and listen to this. She's on vacation, so take all the time you want. I need a minute to handle something here and then I'll check back in with you."

The door was closed on Trevor as he was launching into a brilliant speech about the illegality of taping conversations without someone's prior written consent. Mark wasn't impressed. Line three sounded the "on hold" alarm, so Samantha quickly signed on to her computer and called up her personal Rolodex. The search for Morgan took some time. When the card finally came up on the screen, the line had insistently rang for a second time.

"Oh, shit." she muttered, as she remembered who it was on the phone and could only guess at why he was calling.

Chapter 13

At some point after moving back to Vermont, Samantha began to wonder where her father was and if she would see him again. It wasn't that she had dreams of being reunited with him. On the contrary, she had nightmares about him showing up out of the blue one night, at some client function and embarrassing her. Initially she felt guilty about that. What kind of horrible person was she to pray that her father would never come back?

Remembering what her Grampy had said about guilt, she moved from that temporary state to a different level. Perhaps she was thinking the worst, when maybe he had successfully shed his old life and started a new, rewarding one. She congratulated herself for hoping that this was the case (and not feeling jealous and abandoned because she was not part of it). But gradually the fear of the unknown overtook her. No matter what the cost, she had to find him and make sure that there would be no surprises.

She felt so ridiculous looking through the phone book for a private detective. "Hello? Mr. Rockford? Yes, this is Samantha Armstrong. I'd like you to find my father who disappeared when I was three. Well no, he actually ran away, I guess. Where might he be? Oh I don't know... that was thirty odd years ago and no one has heard from him since. Shall I meet you at your trailer on the beach, so we can discuss your fee? It's so much per day plus expenses, right?"

This was not going to be easy, but she certainly did not have the time or inclination to do the legwork herself. The money was not important; it would be worth it to put her mind at ease.

In her nightmares, Bud always appeared wearing his work clothes from the Mill and looked to be twenty years old, just like Samantha remembered him. It wasn't the young, vibrant athlete whose picture she had seen in that yearbook in the attic. It was a boy with a beaten soul whose dreams had been stolen from him, just as he was about to become a man.

He would be drunk and yell across the room, "Come give your Daddy a kiss, little girl!"

She'd pretend that he was mildly amusing and respond, "Sir, I don't know who you are, but you'll have to leave. This is a private function."

Her clients would shake their heads and trade incredulous comments; their wives would form a semicircle around him and laugh at the two pathetic Vermonters trying "to play" in the world of the rich and famous.

When she awoke from these night terrors, her heart would be pounding in her throat and a sweat like she had just run a marathon would be smothering her body. She'd get up on her hands and knees and start bouncing back and forth on the bed like she was on a rocking horse.

It was something she did every night as a child, to help her fall asleep. At first she did it to drown out the sound of her mother crying in the next room; then it was to shut out the voice of her grandmother; finally it was to break the deadly silence that filled the house when the sun went down.

She had only stopped the ritual when she went away to college. Their first night together, her roommate awoke in the dark and yelled, "What the hell are you doing over there?"

"I dropped something down between the bed and the wall. I was trying to move the bed away from the concrete, so I could reach down and get it... sorry. I'll wait until tomorrow to look for it. Sorry. Night."

"Yeah, whatever... thought you were having sex over there... Forget it. See you in the morning."

It was a good month before she learned to sleep without rocking first. She willed herself to make it through the days even though she was exhausted; however, the minute the lights went out at night, she could feel the resistance return to her body. One day, she discovered that if she just left the television on, she was mercifully able to sleep and all was well in the rocking department from that point forward. That was until the nightmares had started up again back in Vermont.

It seemed strange that she had never feared her father's return at any other important moments in her life. There had been chess tournaments, debate team meets, high school and college graduations after all. Maybe that was because everything prior to that had just been a point on her path to success. Now - she had arrived. Everything was in place. It all came down to control. She had confidence in herself and her abilities; however, she feared that her father or some deep, dark secret from his past could wrestle control away from her and cause her to lose everything.

In any event, after numerous awkward phone conversations and several even stranger person to person meetings, she finally found a man who seemed fairly intelligent and capable of doing what she wanted him to do.

Mr. Wendell was a retired policeman who ran a small investigation service out of his home. Samantha was under the impression that he only took cases that interested him, because money certainly didn't seem to be a motivator. He appeared to enjoy the work of reuniting long lost relatives. His office walls were covered with pictures of smiling former clients. Samantha didn't have the strength to tell him that she was not interested in a similar "happy ending".

It wasn't that Samantha told any lies about her true motives, she just didn't reveal many details. It was enough to get him started to hear the sketchy information that could be provided. For obvious reasons, she was hoping to locate him (unbeknownst to him or any of her other relatives) and then decide how (if?) to approach him. She explained that her maternal Grandmother would be devastated to hear that she was searching for Bud and she didn't want to give his parents false hope; therefore, no one in the Northeast Kingdom must be contacted to assist with the process.

He didn't seem concerned that these conditions would hamper his search. He didn't seem particularly alarmed that there was little information to go on. In fact, he spent a great deal of time going over the various methods he could employ to track a missing person. She was lost about a quarter of the way through phase one, but there was no question of interrupting. Two hours later he stopped talking, so she gratefully took it as a signal that she was free to go.

He promised to keep her updated periodically about his progress and gave her arm a squeeze when they said goodbye in his driveway. "Hang in there - I'll find him for you," were his parting comments.

Exactly one week later, she received a ten-page report. Wendell had traced her father's movements for several years after he left Vermont.

Bud had been quite the traveler. He hadn't stayed in any one place for longer than 8 months. He had made his way through the other New England States and then slowly worked down the East Coast to Florida, where the report ended with a date over five years old.

Not that Samantha had great confidence in the validity of the information before her. How would she know if it were correct or not? Although it hardly made sense to submit so much detail, so soon after their appointment, if Wendell was planning to make up stories to deceive her and bleed her dry with fees and expenses.

No, she felt that the detective she had hired was the real deal. The pit in her stomach grew bigger every day, as she struggled with the question, "Why did I have to open Pandora's Box? My God, what am I going to do if he finds him?"

Chapter 14

The next three months brought no news. Samantha took comfort in the fact that her father wasn't easy to find. Probably he had changed his name or moved to another country. Or maybe he was dead?

She didn't call Wendell for an update. Her theory was no news is good news. Just when she had gone a day or two without thinking about it, the detective came to see her at CRS unannounced. This annoyed her, since she hardly wanted any of her staff to see him or question why he was there.

Luckily she was standing in the reception area as he walked in, so she simply greeted him and quickly directed him into her office.

"Well this is a surprise..."

"I apologize for not calling," he smiled, "but, I thought—"

"I don't like surprises," she retorted.

Wendell was so excited about his news, he didn't even realize that she was already displeased with him. "I've been hoping like hell that something would break and I'd be able to give you more, but I've just hit a brick wall."

"Mr. Wendell, I appreciate your dedication, but certainly I understand that there is only so much you can do."

"Well it's not that. I mean, there's more I can do - I think. I'd like to go down to Florida myself and dig around."

The last sentence was delivered staccato and the only thing she could think of to say was, "What?"

"I want to go down to Florida myself to pick up the scent. I know it's been five years, but there's a pattern here and I think I can crack the code and find him for you. I know that's what you want more than anything. And I want to be able to do that for you."

Was that really what she wanted? And if so, was it worth the risk?

In the end, she had said yes and Wendell was on his way to sunny Florida. One month later he called from Boston. He had good news and bad news.

Being the pessimist that she was, she asked for the bad news first. "Your father is a homeless person, who doesn't have a clue what his name is or where he's from. And... he's... dying."

"Oh, I see. Wendell?"

"Yeah?"

"What's the good news?"

"I found him."

Chapter 15

Well. That was that. She could have saved herself the trouble. He wasn't in Vermont, he had no clue who he was and he wasn't long for this world.

She should have felt relieved, but she didn't. Instead, it felt like a giant burden had fallen down from the sky and landed square on her shoulders. Now what the hell was she supposed to do?

Chapter 16

The plan came together quickly enough. She couldn't recall if it was one hundred percent her idea or if Wendell had a hand in crafting the scheme. It didn't matter. As with most things in her life these days, she got what she wanted out of the arrangement.

She supplied all the funds needed for Wendell to transfer her father from his street corner in Boston to a private nursing home outside Elkin and she would continue to pay the bills for his around the clock care. It was a great deal more than she had imagined, but it was the least she could do.

She had decided long ago that she would never visit him. If he had been healthy, she honestly did not know how she would have reacted; however, given his mental state, there really was no point. Nothing could be gained by seeing him in that condition. She would simply remain in the background as his silent benefactor. Maybe the rest of his family would be able to recapture some peace of mind by knowing that he would at least die in as much comfort as possible.

Wendell was to notify her Grandparents that their long lost son had been found and ensconced in the nearby facility, at the expense of the United States Government. Samantha told the detective to prepare an elaborate story to explain that thanks to Bud's incredible service and sacrifice in the Armed Forces in Vietnam, there would be no charges to the family.

When this last task was completed, Samantha thanked Wendell with a large bonus and felt a tinge of guilt when she saw the tears welling up in his eyes. He surveyed the wide array of photographs around his office and murmured, "I'm sorry that I didn't find him soon enough for your happy ending."

"Well you know what they say... It's never too late," she whispered as she lowered her head and left him behind reliving happier moments from his professional career.

Ever since then, she had sent a check to the Sunset Village Nursing Home once a month for her father's maintenance. Wendell had asked the Director to report to Samantha whenever Bud received visitors. Not once had she been called with the news that anyone had bothered to travel the ten miles or so to see him since his return from Massachusetts. One time however, a Mr. Morgan had sent a note to let her know that he had not forgotten the task, it was simply a matter of fact that no one ever came.

Mr. Morgan. That's who was on the phone. Good Lord, did he think she cared now if someone finally showed up to read her father the riot act about disappearing three decades ago? Or could it be that her transparent cover had been blown and someone figured out that Bud had never served his country anywhere, least of all in Vietnam? What difference could any of this make? He wouldn't be calling to suggest that she should visit, would he?

The thought occurred to her that she hadn't eaten anything in a very long time, but she desperately wanted to vomit. Instead, she took a deep breath, picked up the receiver and punched the flashing light. "Samantha

Armstrong." Silence greeted her for so long that she was tempted to hang up.

"Oh, Ms. Armstrong, yes, sorry to keep you waiting." Was he being facetious? Samantha wondered, somewhat annoyed, but in the next moment everything but his words were forgotten.

"This is Mr. Morgan from Sunset Village. I'm sorry to bother you, but I thought that you would like to know immediately. Your father passed away twenty minutes ago. I'm very sorry."

She knew why cartoon characters saw stars when they passed out. That's what it was like for her. Her office seemed suddenly so bright that she had to squint to see. It felt like her head was too big for her neck. Why didn't she have any control over her body? Her eyes were still not focusing, as she stared out the glass partition into the reception area. Everything was moving in slow motion. Mark was coming from the back hallway, with a disgusted look on his face, but he looked like a runner from those sequences in the movie "Chariots of Fire".

She had never fainted before, but there's a first time for everything.

Chapter 17

She must have hit the corner of the computer stand when she went down. Gradually awakening, she noticed there were too many people in her office and they were all shouting at each other to remain calm. There seemed to be blood everywhere and she had a feeling it had originated from her head.

Someone was holding a towel over her eye and her assistant was trying to crawl over everyone and everything to get to the rest of the telephone, which had fallen down behind the credenza.

They could hear Mr. Morgan yelling, "Hello? Is anyone there? What's going on? Hello?" but no one could get the cord untwisted and the receiver pulled back up.

"Put the call on hold and go pick it up at another workstation," Samantha sputtered as she grabbed the soaked rag off her wound and slapped the helping hand away from her.

Everyone stopped and stared for about three seconds and then someone said, "I think she's going to be alright." It was at that point that the whole room erupted in a laughter that was half relief and half wonder at what would come next in this most unusual day.

Mark shooed everyone out of the room and then closed the door. "Are you ok?"

"Yes. I feel so stupid! I've never in my life done that before."

"What happened?"

"Nothing. No big deal. Really. Nothing. But, never mind about that... Did you listen to the tape?" She could tell by the way his face fell that he had.

"I'm sorry, Mark. He just made me so mad, I had to find a way to put him in his place. I certainly understand if you never want to do business with me again. It's been quite a day."

"Ms. Armstrong, you are something else. I want to thank you. Just when I thought I knew it all, you go and pull my rose colored glasses off. I've been an old fool with that kid, but thanks to you I think there's time to turn things around. Of course I still want you to handle my affairs - Are you crazy? Wait. You better not answer that!"

They both laughed. "Mark, thanks for everything. You've been great, as always. Normally I would stay around and make sure that you had all that you wanted before your flight, but I've got to confess that the phone call I got was some rather bad news."

She noted the look of deep concern on his ruggedly handsome face and she silently wished that he had fired her, so she could ask him out. When he started to open his mouth to ask, she held up her hand and shook her head. "It's ok. I'll be fine. It was expected, but you know, even when it's for the best, it's still a shock."

She had no idea if he had any clue as to what she was referring. But she was glad he didn't ask and therefore she didn't have to tell. And she was very grateful to Mark Monahan for that. More grateful than he would ever know.

Chapter 18

Samantha called Mr. Morgan back within the hour and explained (as best she could) what had transpired earlier. They discussed some of the arrangements and she promised to meet with him in the morning.

Then she went home. She hadn't told anyone why. The staff was simply informed that she would be out for two or three days and unavailable during that time. She had delivered the news with anxiety, expecting to see fear in their faces. Instead, she could have sworn that she noticed something closer to excitement in the looks that were almost imperceptibly exchanged. They were excited at the thought of being on their own without her supervision. Go figure.

Chapter 19

God she wished Jeannie were here. She had no idea what to pack. What would be appropriate for the funeral? After standing in front of her closet and looking at everything hanging there at least three times, she finally realized that she didn't give a damn what she was supposed to wear. She placed her bright red tailored suit in her overnight case and started to laugh. If anyone bothered to show up, wouldn't her outfit get the town's tongues wagging?

* *

As she drove down the Interstate towards Montpelier, she didn't feel any different than if she were heading to the Insurance Department to meet with the Director of Captives.

It was only as she made her way through the capitol and kept going on Route 2 that the knot in her stomach began to overtake her. She tried to take deep, relaxing breaths, but the discomfort grew.

She started talking to herself in East Montpelier and by the time she reached Plainfield, she was positively babbling. What was she doing? Why was she even bothering to go make final arrangements for a man who had abandoned her? And her Mother... Wasn't he basically responsible for her Mother's suicide? He had chosen to throw his life away, much like his young wife - just using a different method.

An image of a lone coffin in a darkened room formed in her mind. She was there with her Father, all dressed up in her favorite suit (his favorite color had been red also), sitting quietly in a chair as the visiting hours came and went with not one interruption. Why would there be? No one had come to see him since she had moved him to the nursing home. She had made sure that everyone who could have had an interest in the news was informed. No one had come. Not even his parents, her Grandparents. Why was that? Would they come to the funeral home? Did she want them to? She didn't even know anymore what she wanted.

When she greeted Mr. Morgan he offered his sympathies and informed her that he had started making the arrangements with a reputable Funeral Home in town. She thought his choice of words had been odd, but then she remembered the scandal that had broken in the Burlington Free Press a few months back about improper handling of bodies by a local Funeral Parlor.

She was soon of the opinion that proper handling wasn't all that it was cracked up to be. Since she had been so young when her Mother had died and had not returned home when her Grandfather had passed, this aspect was something she was totally unfamiliar with. The whole process made her violently ill.

Whenever the owner of the Funeral Home spoke with her she wanted to slap him. His soft voice and the look of constant concern plastered to his face made her wonder how anyone could possibly do this for a living. She understood that not many found Insurance

Accounting as stimulating as she did; however, who in their right mind would enjoy being around the dead and their mourning relatives day in and day out? And if one started out in one's right mind, how in God's name could you stay there? The whole thing was so creepy.

It wasn't long before her true feelings became known. There was a definite change in attitude and a move from patience, sympathy and understanding to expediency. She was not cheap in her arrangements, just efficient and realistic. Did he need the most comfortable fabric and box design? No. Would he have visiting hours and a funeral mass? Yes. Would anyone else feel him deserving? She would know within 24 hours.

Chapter 20

She was pleased to see that there were several Motels to choose from in the area. Coming over she had panicked that she hadn't called her travel agent to reserve a room. By the time she had driven through town though, she had already seen three vacancy signs.

Since she seemed to have time, she decided to walk back along Main Street. So many of the structures were just as she remembered from her childhood visits to the big city of Elkin. Some of the grand houses had been fixed up in those intervening years; others had fallen into disrepair. She surveyed the Academy at the end of the road and was impressed with the changes she saw there. It looked like a small college campus. It really was a beautiful place, but it held too many painful memories for her and her family.

She remembered the determination of one lonely little girl who couldn't wait to graduate and leave this town behind her forever. It wasn't that she had vowed never to return, but she certainly thought that she had seen the last of this place a long time ago.

When the cold and hungry signals finally reached her brain, it was too late. She had foolishly left her car back at the funeral home, while she took this ridiculous stroll down memory lane. She was tired too. All she wanted was a nice warm bed, with a tray from room service. She had a feeling that Elkin hadn't changed that much. Either she was going to a grocery store or going out to a restaurant - room service was not an option.

The grocery store won out, but then she couldn't decide what to buy. It seemed that everything needed to be prepared, refrigerated and/or put in a microwave. In the end, she grabbed a bag of Oreos and a carton of milk and headed to the most luxurious of the accommodations she had seen on the way into town that day.

The room wasn't really that bad and the bed was very comfortable. She ate a whole sleeve of the cookies, drank all the milk and then fell into a deep sleep. She awoke feeling refreshed and started to smile, until she remembered what day it was.

She would bury her father today. She had given up on looking for a happy ending long ago, but at least this was an end. She could start over. She would finally be free of her past. But no matter how many times she told herself that, the overpowering feeling that today was no different than any other day would not go away. She wasn't scared by that thought - just damn exhausted.

Chapter 21

The suit looked good on her. The makeup job she had done wasn't bad either. Was food served at the visiting hours? Probably not, since she hadn't picked out a menu, along with the hundred or so other details she had mulled over. She was starving, but she couldn't bear the thought of eating anything other than the Oreos. Hopefully this would go away in a day or two.

She took her time driving to the funeral home, as she was in no rush to start her lonely vigil. She parked her car amid the many in the lot, wondering whose visiting hours were before her father's. Must be people had stayed over.

When she entered the front room, her trusty new best friend, Mr. Bayer, greeted her with the same pained expression she had come to expect. Maybe some people in her situation found it comforting, but it annoyed Samantha.

"I'm sorry. Am I disturbing another service?"

"No, of course not. Your father's friends started arriving about 15 minutes ago. There's quite a crowd in the main room and I believe there is even some spill over into the second sitting room. He must have been a popular man."

Just as she was about to shake her head and say, "Excuse me?" she heard a wail erupt from the next room. The hair on the back of her neck bristled as her mind raced back to Silver

Pond. The day when she had last heard that cry.

She walked over to the guest book and turned to the front page. She knew what the first listing would be before she read it. She'd know that sound and whom it originated from anywhere. It was her Grandmother-the woman who had cried out like that when she had found her Daughter-in-law hanging from the rafters. Her name was signed first in the pretty little book that had cost $22. But who were all these other people and why were they here? No one had come to visit him when he was alive. What were they doing here now? It was going to be a very long day...

Chapter 22

She had to grip the podium that held the book, so that she wouldn't fall over. For some reason her legs had turned into jelly and she was unable to move from the spot.

Mr. Bayer was busy greeting other mourners as they came in, skillfully steering them away from Samantha and directly into the main room.

After several minutes he was back at her side. "I know this is very difficult for you, Ms. Armstrong, but if you are ready, everyone is waiting." He reached out for her elbow, presumably to guide her into the other room, but she managed to move away before he could touch her.

"What in God's name are you talking about?" she hissed through clenched teeth. For a moment, Mr. Bayer was taken aback.

"Well... as his daughter, you should be there before the memorial service starts. Of course." He added the last part with a slight shake of his head, as if everyone knew that.

"Mr. Bayer, I appreciate the fact that you are quite familiar with this area - this business - processing the dead, or whatever you want to call it; however, please be advised that I have no familiarity with it at all. It is completely and utterly foreign to me and I don't have a clue what I should be doing (according to custom, that is) or what I want to do (given the circumstances of my father's life and death)."

For once he seemed to be at a loss for words. His expression changed to one of confusion and he bit his lower lip as he pondered what to do next.

"Ummmm... Do you want me to delay the prayer session... or..." his voice trailed off as he realized that she wasn't going to answer.

"What did I just say? I don't know! To be honest, I'd like to run out that door and leave you to do whatever the hell all those jokers in that room want you to do."

Mr. Bayer took a giant step backward and put a hand to his chest in disbelief. "Ms. Armstrong!"

"Oh, please! Give me a break. You of all people must have seen more than your share of (here she put both arms in the air and made the quotation mark gesture with the first two fingers of each hand) mourners that were submitting Academy Award winning performances!"

He took a deep breath, closed his eyes and tilted his head downward for several seconds before looking back up at her. "Grief is a funny thing, Ms. Armstrong. Everyone handles it in their own way. I'm sorry for your loss." And then he was gone.

Should she go after him and explain why this whole afternoon was a farce? No. She would never see him again and didn't care what he did or did not understand about her unique situation. It was time to make a decision. She could leave and be done with it all or she could march into the next room and confront those hypocrites.

It was no secret what her beloved Grandfather would have done. He wouldn't have wasted his time with the idiots in the other room, sharing memories of things that never happened, patting each other on the back to distill those horrible feelings of guilt.

"Don't waste your time going to a funeral, Blossum" she could hear him saying, "Do something else that you love, or better yet, something that he loved."

What exactly would that be? Something that he loved. He deserted her Mother. He hadn't bothered to keep tabs on her or his parents throughout the years. He liked his booze, but Samantha never drank. She had to admit she knew nothing about the corpse in the next room. If possible, she knew even less now, then she did before she embarked on the journey to find him.

This was the end. She couldn't run away now. She signed her name in the book and then stepped back, handing the pen to the young couple that had just come in. They smiled and she returned it, albeit briefly. One more lean against the stairwell to regain her strength and then she pushed off and marched into the next room.

She was not prepared for what came next. This couldn't be right! People were milling around, some standing in groups of two or three, while others huddled by some chairs that lined the near wall. On the far wall was an open coffin with a shriveled up old man displayed for all to see. She looked around in disbelief, waiting for everyone else to notice that a dead man was among them. No one seemed fazed by the spectacle. What was wrong with these people???

"S-A-M-A-N-T-H-A, darling" was called from far away and she saw an even older, female version of the deceased making her way through the crowd. Her grandmother was dressed in black from the hat on her head to the old pumps on her feet. "Where's the fire," she whispered in her ear as she gave her a hug and then held her at arms length to get a good look at the suit she disapproved of.

"Hello." It was all she could manage to say. She wanted to scream, "Where the fuck were you when he was alive? Living a measly nine miles away from you? You couldn't go visit him then, but you can come here now with all your friends and cry for him? You make me sick. I hate you and all that you stand for."

The initial urge she had to slap her was quick to depart, when she took in the devastating toll that time had already taken. Her grandmother was quick to dry her tears and start making her way back through the crowds with Samantha in tow. She was being introduced to people left and right with lines like, "You remember John. Oh, here's Gary. And Fred, how nice of you to come. This is my Granddaughter, Samantha." Each time she was greeted with a quick intake of breath and a nod of encouragement. Apparently she was extremely lucky that all these people knew exactly how she felt and were "there" for her.

The young people in attendance were either friends or neighbors of her Grandmother or distant relatives that she had never met. Samantha couldn't help but wonder if it was some sort of Vermont Holiday that all these strangers could take time off work to attend a memorial service for someone they couldn't possibly have known.

The walk through the room was excruciatingly slow. Her head was spinning with names, faces and empty cliches. The temperature in the house was stifling. What a mistake her choice of clothing was. She desperately wanted to take off her jacket, but the moisture she felt underneath her arms suggested it was too late.

When there were no more visitors to greet, she gratefully accepted her Grandmother's suggestion to sit down and get caught up. It only took a few questions for Samantha to realize that her Grandmother was trapped in a time warp. It was as if the last 15 years did not exist. Other than a snide comment about how well she must be doing (accompanied by a raised eyebrow and another disgusted glance at her apparel) she didn't ask about where she had disappeared to or why.

In return, Samantha did not ask anything of substance. There were comments about the weather, the crowd and how nice Mr. Bayer was. No questions about why she never visited her son after he was found and brought back to her. No comments about how much she was overreacting today to his expected death.

Their talk was interrupted for the service. Oddly it was the only part of the day that seemed to fly by. It was over before she expected.

Her Grandmother hugged her goodbye and stated that she would see her at home. There was no uncertainty about whether Samantha would come or not. It was expected. It was tradition. It was the way things were done.

After everyone else had gone, she knelt in front of the casket. She did not know how to finish this part. Even now, knowing that she would never see him again, she couldn't bear to touch him. Her hand stroking the side of his final resting place, she closed her eyes and whispered, "I hope you've found peace."

Quickly, she stood up, straightened her skirt and then headed for the door. At the front of the room, she turned and said with difficulty, "Goodbye, Daddy." With her hand on the doorknob she heard a noise and then felt a presence behind her. It was Bayer.

"Goodbye, Ms. Armstrong. Again, I'm sorry for your loss." This time he didn't have the usual sympathetic look on his face, but rather an expression of utter disgust. Whereas moments earlier she had feared an onslaught of tears, she now felt back in control of her emotions.

"Well Bayer, you know what they say... my loss is your gain. Hope we don't cross paths again, you sick bastard."

She slammed the door in his stunned face and then took a deep breath. She had made it through that ordeal, how much harder could it be to go to her Grandmother's house and say goodbye to all the rest? How much harder indeed...

Chapter 23

She sat in her car for several minutes contemplating her next move. It involved going to her grandmother's house, as she had already decided on the script for her performance there. But she was torn between the idea of going back to the Motel, showering and changing her clothes or heading straight over to end this ordeal as soon as possible.

Because she was so uncomfortable, a hot shower won out. The water felt wonderful and she could feel the tension leaving her body. This was going to be a piece of cake. She could see the light at the end of the tunnel now and it was pure heaven.

She confidently changed into more inappropriate dress and headed in the direction of her grandparent's house out Eastern Avenue. It was a beautiful ride; she just wished that she could keep going for hours and enjoy the scenery. What a gorgeous place this was. If things had been different, she might have lived in one of these grand old houses with a handsome husband and a passel of children. Of course that would have brought other problems. Things would have been different, but who is to say that she would have been any better off in the long run?

In fact, she was doing quite well anyway. She was successful. And happy, wasn't she? If not, would she be in a couple of hours? Was saying goodbye to some old haunts from the past the only thing standing in her way? She would soon find out.

The house hadn't changed that much. She pulled in the driveway and sat in the car watching the people through the windows. There were little children running from the kitchen out onto the new deck and then jumping onto the grass below. They were laughing and screaming and totally enjoying their play together, oblivious to why all the adults were gathered inside.

But then again, the adults seemed to be enjoying themselves as well. There was laughter coming from inside and it seemed that plenty of eating was involved too. She now found that her appetite had returned. Maybe she could prepare a plate to go.

Samantha watched in the rear view mirror as a truck pulled in behind her and the somber couple emerged with a crock of what had to be baked beans. They entered through the front door and made their way through the house giving hugs and kisses as they went. She could see that once the kitchen was reached, the mood was decidedly different. Obviously she would have to deliver her soliloquy in the living room to take advantage of the depressed setting.

Two or three families were loading up their belongings in their vehicles, getting ready to head out, so Samantha thought it was time. She made her way to the front door, rehearsing one more time the words that would be her last to these people. The calm from the Motel was no more, but it was replaced with an energy that she found exhilarating.

"Darling, you made it," was her grandmother's greeting, "and thank God you changed! This outfit is still a bit much, but I'll take it sweet pea." She giggled, wrapped her arms around Samantha and gave a weak squeeze.

The overpowering scent of her perfume was revolting, but it served to strengthen her resolve.

"Look who is here everyone... our famous granddaughter, Samantha. Come all the way from the big city to comfort us in our hour of need. Bless you honey."

It was the perfect opening that Samantha had prayed for. "Speaking of hours of need, Grammy, I'm a little curious. Was my Father ill long?"

The room went stone silent. Anyone who had been facing Samantha stopped what they were doing and simply stared at her. The others that had been turned away just stood still. Afraid to move a muscle and risk becoming involved in where this question would inevitably lead, they chose instead to look either at the ceiling or the floor.

"Oh precious. Your Daddy was so - troubled - from the day he met your Mother. It was only a matter of time before he self destructed."

Samantha could not believe her ears. "Yes, I see what you mean. It's hardly been, what? Forty years!?!? But I actually wasn't referring to his - trouble. I'm more interested in how he had been since moving to Sunset Village."

"Oh, yes. A lovely place. Bud never said much, but we think he liked it. Poor thing would have been so hurt if he had known how much money it was costing us to keep him there in comfort."

Even though she had expected a statement along these lines at some point, she thought she would at least have to work for it. It had been too easy. Had her Grandmother read her mind? No, of course not, or she would be cowering in fear for what was coming next.

"Of course, I didn't think what a financial burden you must have had to deal with. Grandmother, I'm sorry. I guess I should have been helping you with that."

"We didn't want to trouble you, deary. Your father was so proud of you and didn't want you to be bothered with his situation. He'd be happy to know that you are here now though and that you'll be taking care of me right proper."

"So he talked about me often?"

"Oh yes. Every Sunday."

Samantha knew that this was pure fabrication. The only question was: Did her Grandmother believe it too? Was she as nutty as her son had been?

"I see. And when did he take a turn for the worst?"

"Oh, I don't know exactly. A gradual decline I guess. How long does it take to die from a broken heart?" Mrs. Armstrong mistook the look Samantha shot her as one of regret and quickly added, "Now, now. No need to blame yourself dear. We all did the best we could."

The bitterness and hatred that was welling up in Samantha was only controlled by sitting down at the desk before her and clenching her teeth. She opened her pocketbook and took out her checkbook. She saw her Grandmother's whole face light up and then be toned down for effect. "Well I guess I'm starting to feel that perhaps I could have done more. Especially with the expenses, since I am doing so well."

Here she looked around the room and saw that the rest of the people had turned to face her and many were mumbling and nodding their heads. "Grammy, what would you say would be a fair reimbursement to you, for my share of Father's medical bills?"

"Oh honey, that is so sweet. Did you hear that everyone? Do I have the best Granddaughter in the world, or what?" Again, her guests nodded their agreement. "Don't worry about me. What do I need this big old house for anyway? I can always sell it and move into town. Before long, you'll have to have me set up there in Sunset Village."

"Now, now. Don't talk like that Mrs. Armstrong," said a young woman who moved in beside her to take the spot that Samantha had occupied. She put her arm around her shoulders and gave her a kiss. This time the chorus was shaking their heads and making stronger rumblings.

"Well tell you what. I've got to be going, so I'm just going to throw out a figure. How's $75,000 sound?"

There were quick intakes of breath and several more people sat down around them. "Samantha. You're being a little crass, don't you think?" She said the words through a smile, but it was obvious that her embarrassment was growing.

Samantha had no doubt that the only thing that her Grandmother objected to was announcing the amount in front of the whole town. Well let's see how she liked part two.

"You know what. That's not really fair is it? You were here with him all this time. Suffering as he suffered. Dealing with the tremendous guilt he must have had concerning my mother's suicide. Although I'm sure he tried to unload a lot of that on you, since you raised such a pathetic coward!"

"Samantha! What are you saying?" Several bystanders lunged to catch Mrs. Armstrong, as she slumped towards the floor.

"I'm saying, what the hell? How about I make it a good $250,000 and we call it even?"

"Well that is very generous, but I must say that I am finding your attitude quite distasteful. This might be the way you young people from the city do business, but you're back in the country now missy. You better show some respect for your elders."

Samantha finished making the check out, slammed the cover shut and threw it back into her pocketbook. She smiled and handed the check to her Grandmother who was alternating between salivating and acting indignant.

"I must say you deserve it. Can't say I'll be back this way again, because I won't. As far as I'm concerned, all of you can go to Hell. And why don't you say hello to my Father when you get there?"

There was a small cry from Mrs. Armstrong when she saw that the check was made out to A Lying Bitch.

"By the way, you made a few mistakes," said Samantha as she turned smiling at the door, "see I'm the one who tracked my Father down in Boston and had him moved here. So he could be close to you; so you all could spend as much time as you wanted with him in the end. I paid for his care, not you, not the Government, not insurance - me. And we all know that you spent exactly as much time as you wanted to with him, didn't you? Which was no time. Not one minute. You people are pathetic!"

"SAMANTHA!"

She heard her name as the door slammed shut. There was something in the tone that made her go back in the house, instead of run to the car like every fiber in her being was telling her to do.

Her Grandmother had a wild look on her face as she ripped the check to shreds and then tried to throw it at her. It didn't go very far at all, simply fluttered to the floor around her feet.

"You think you're so smart, don't you, you ungrateful..." her Grandmother's voice trailed off as she stomped down the hall towards the bedrooms. Samantha was unsure if her Grandmother intended to come back, so she started to leave again.

"You think you know everything, huh? How it was my son that killed your Mother, huh? Well guess again. Here - take it... I don't want it anymore." She threw an old yellowed envelope at her and after juggling it two or three times, Samantha finally got a grip on it. When she could look at it, she saw her name written in faded ink on the front.

That feeling of exhilaration, that thought that she was seconds away from freedom disappeared in the time it took for her Grandmother to laugh, "Why it's your Mother's suicide note, my darling! I've kept it all these years to protect you. Because I loved you and thought you loved me. Fine, you have no use for your father or me, God Bless you. But do not stand there and tell me that he was responsible for her death. I think you are going to be quite surprised by the truth. Now get out of my house!"

"Why did you—"

"I said to get the Hell out of my house. I never want to see you again. You can rot in

Hell for all I care. You and your slut Mother deserved each other. I'm glad my son got out when he did. He deserved better. He would have been something. He was talented. He would have..."

Samantha didn't hear anymore. She put the envelope in her pocket and walked out. For the first time in her life her car wouldn't start, but she knew it was only because she was trying too hard. She hit the steering wheel with the heel of her hand a few times to compose herself and then started it with a vengeance. She threw it into reverse and flew out of the driveway. The oncoming car swerved around her, but she was oblivious to the reaction she had provoked.

Her mind was spinning. What was her Grandmother talking about? Why did she have her Mother's suicide note? How did she get it? The police never found one and had said that often there is no such thing. Had she made it up? If so, she would have had to long ago, as it certainly seemed the right age and look for something that old. Beyond that, there was one question burning more intently than all the others combined - What did the note say?

Chapter 24

She drove recklessly down the highway, heading back to town. Several times she took corners too wide and caused other drivers a few moments of panic. About half way back to the Motel, she pulled over quickly and jumped out of the car.

Her head was filled with images and voices that she could not bear right now. A few minutes ago, she thought she was saying goodbye to the last ghost from her past. Now she felt like a helpless little girl again, reliving that day of her Mother's suicide.

She leaned against the car and closed her eyes tight. There it was, the scream from inside the house. She could feel herself running and then she saw her Mother dangling from the rafter. But wait, everything is different this time. In the chair below is an envelope with "Samantha" written on it. It's a note that will explain everything. It will all make sense now. She won't have to feel responsible anymore, because her Mother is finally going to answer all her questions. In her mind, she opens the envelope and everyone else in the room disappears. The warmth leaves her body as she looks down and sees that the page is blank. Nothing has changed after all.

Chapter 25

She gently removed the envelope from her pocket and got back into the car. She held it in firm hands, sensing that it might be powerful enough to leap out of them if she didn't. It wasn't a very thick envelope, probably only one piece of paper. Did it have writing on both sides? Would it bring her peace or torment? Why did her Grandmother hold it all these years, but decide to give it to her now?

Samantha was afraid. It was obvious that the contents were going to affect her deeply and from what her Grandmother had said, not in a comforting way.

Suddenly she was very tired. The note would have to go back in her pocket for safekeeping. Back in control of her emotions, she could drive at a reasonable pace without offending any more motorists today.

She reached the Motel and dragged herself into the room. Without even turning on a light or the television, she fell into bed and immediately slept. It was a blessing. She awoke with the thought that there had been no dreams or nightmares for a change. It was a new day, but what would she do with it?

Chapter 26

It was time to return to Burlington. She wasn't sure what to do about the note, but she wanted desperately to get back to work and some sort of familiar routine.

She was very hungry, but didn't bother to stop anywhere after checking out. As opposed to the two or three restaurant choices available here, just waiting ninety minutes would bring thirty times that amount.

The trip back was uneventful, which made it pleasant. She was so thrilled to be home that she didn't even mind that Jeannie wasn't there.

Chapter 27

"You have quite a few messages on your desk," was her secretary's greeting the next morning when Samantha arrived at CRS. "Those are the ones that can wait; these are the ones that are urgent." Samantha smiled when she was handed some twenty odd pink slips of paper - God it was great to be back.

Before she could relax and enjoy it however, she needed to get the ball rolling on something else. Somewhere between leaving her Grandmother's house and returning to her own, she realized that her personal affairs needed some attention. She motioned for her secretary to follow her into the office and then closed the door as she took a seat.

"I want you to call Carlene Dugan over at Upton Sheltra ASAP. See if she can recommend someone to handle a special matter for me - preparing a... well taking care of my, my will."

The look of alarm that came over her face was almost comical. "Don't worry, I'm not planning on checking out anytime soon. It's just time I acknowledged that I'm not immortal. I have certain wishes that must be arranged for. I'm not sure who I want my things to go to, but I'll be damned if they'll go to anyone in my family, simply because I was too lazy to make sure they didn't!

"Anyway, see if Carlene can set me up for a lunch meeting (you know that cafe on the first floor of their new building downtown) with someone - today - she owes me for the United Services referral."

She shooed her secretary toward the door - she had her assignment and Samantha wanted to get at least half of these emergencies handled before lunch. It was important for her clients to realize that she was back and service would be better than ever. She almost believed that herself, except for the feeling that a dark cloud was lingering behind her, waiting to engulf her in more tragedy.

Before leaving the house that morning, she had moved the envelope to her pocketbook. It was now sitting in the bottom right hand desk drawer. What harm would it do to leave it where it was? What harm would it do to read it and be done with it? She had lived all these years without the benefit of its contents, why risk her sanity by revealing her Mother's secrets now? If only her Grandmother hadn't thrown the note at her with such hatred and self-satisfaction. She knew it was her hope that the revelations would be devastating. Samantha couldn't help running through a million "if onlys" in her head. If only her Grandmother didn't already know what was in there. If only she hadn't gone to her Grandmother's house. If only she hadn't gone to the funeral. If only she had never found her father. If only...

Chapter 28

Mark was unavailable when she called his office, his message being the top priority in the stack in front of her. Samantha said a little prayer for this small blessing, then told Patrice, his loyal right hand, that she was back in the office for good. Mark should feel free to call her whenever he got a chance; however, it wasn't necessary if the only purpose was to check up on her health and well being. The bitch is back, is what she left as the message.

As long as she had known Mark and weathered every crisis under the sun with Patrice: his heart attack during a takeover of a rival firm, his wife's affair after thirty years of supposed marital bliss, his inability to keep any key employee in his inner circle for more than two years, a major investment debacle, etc., it was hard for her to believe that she had never met Patrice. And she had no clue what she looked like. She ran his office from the home base and never traveled with him. No need, since they were in constant contact via cell phone. It was actually that way for a lot of Samantha's clients. The Captive business lent itself quite well to service via fax, phone and overnight mail.

She reminded herself again that it was a good life and tackled the next four pink slips. Oh no. Mrs. Munson's Alzheimer's must be acting up again. The first note was a reminder for Samantha that the Annual Meeting had to be at the airport this year, as the people flying in from Pierre only had a half hour before their connecting flight to Boston. Of course if it hadn't been for the requirement that they physically meet in Vermont at least once a year, the circuitous route wouldn't even have been suggested. The second note was a question for Samantha - Had she heard anything about this year's annual meeting with the people from Pierre? The third communication was another question: The clients from Pierre had already met in Vermont once this year, right? Their obligation was fulfilled? The final note of the grouping urged Samantha to contact Julie, as there seemed to be some confusion as to when the Annual Meeting was this year.

Samantha made a quick call to Julie, Beverly Munson's secretary, who had the unfortunate task of trying to rein in her confused mother-in-law. It was soon verified that the Munsons had not regained the Pierre account, which had been lost over five years ago. She was aware that the Portland people were arriving the day after tomorrow and appropriate arrangements had been made at the hotel of their choice. No small task to remember everyone's favorite home away from home, but it was one of the many perks of dealing with Samantha's firm. She never forgot a small detail like that and maintained wonderful relationships with all the hospitality providers within a fifteen-mile radius of the office.

She allowed herself a brief chuckle, as she knew from experience that it would only be a few minutes before Mrs. Munson called back to start the whole cycle over again. That reminded her. Something else to put on her checklist to discuss with the lawyer. "If my mind goes before my body, please arrange to have me bumped off!"

The next three messages were what Samantha considered real emergencies and barked orders to five different associates to get possible solutions in order for some sizable changes in the plans of operation for two major clients. This required her to make several calls to Montpelier. One was to the Director of Captives, the next to the Chief Examiner and finally one to the Commissioner of Banking and Insurance. Since the final conversation was the most successful, she wished that she had handled that one first and built up momentum from there. The Chief Examiner had some concerns that did need to be addressed, but the Director was in no mood to be toyed with today. Best to call him back tomorrow, when Samantha had more information to share with him.

And so it went for three straight hours. Calls, faxes and mail came and went and the stacks on her desk were methodically attacked, so the materials could be disbursed throughout the office. She had completely forgotten about lunch, when she was buzzed with instructions to meet Tim Shepherd from Upton Sheltra in the cafe in twenty-five minutes.

She needed to get gas before she met with him, so she took one more glance around the office and headed out, pocketbook in hand. This must be a record. She hadn't thought about THE ENVELOPE (as she had come to call it) from the point that she had returned to work. That weird feeling came back to the pit of her stomach, assuring her that a long-term solution needed to be devised very soon. This would not be a planning lunch; it would be a "let's work out all the nitty, gritty details today, so we both can be done with this nonsense permanently" meeting.

As she pulled into the parking garage she swore under her breath. She had forgotten to get gas, but looking in her rear view mirror it was obvious that there was no place to go but in. Three cars and their harried drivers were already on her tail. Even though she could have driven all around the first floor and then checked out with the attendant, she didn't feel like dealing with one of his stupid woman jokes today. It probably wouldn't help if she retorted with, "I'm sorry, did you flunk the exam to park cars in college, so they only let you sit in the booth?" so she took the first spot available on the right hand side and locked up.

The elevator seemed to take forever, but finally she was released from the compartment and could head into the restaurant. She twisted her ankle coming around the corner, but managed to catch herself on the doorway. Looking up she saw Carlene Dugan standing next to a table in the middle of the room.

Sunlight filtered down from the Greenhouse ceiling, enveloping the man that Carlene was talking with. He smiled as he caught Samantha's gaze and she had to use her hold on the doorjamb to support herself. She could feel the color rising to her cheeks and felt the need to touch one, just to verify that it was not on fire. For the second time in her life she thought she would faint. She didn't. In front of her was the most incredible looking man that she had ever seen. "If there is a God," she muttered, "that creature will be Mr. Tim Shepherd and I will be spending the next hour and a half with him. If there is not a God, somebody please bump me off NOW."

Chapter 29

Her legs weren't functioning very well as she walked toward the duo. Carlene made a face and looked at her watch when she noticed Samantha coming.

"Hi Samantha, I'm so sorry, you just missed Tim," she said and turned toward the window, as if to say he left the restaurant via a rope ladder dangled from a helicopter. She grasped Samantha's outstretched hand and shook vigorously. "God it's good to see you, how are you?"

Samantha could feel the man's eyes on her (Damn, he wasn't the lawyer she was supposed to meet!) and knew that he was just as anxiously awaiting an introduction as she was.

Before Samantha could stop her, Carlene launched into a lengthy explanation about Tim's whereabouts. It didn't matter. She couldn't recall why she had come here, but knew that she was about to meet the man of her dreams. "Carlene, not a problem, don't worry about it. We can do it another time." She missed the confused look on Carlene's face, because she turned toward the man who was waiting patiently next to her.

"Please don't let me interrupt you any more, Mr...?" She was surprised to find the man was much older than she had initially thought; in fact, she would use the word old to describe him. But as he took her hand in his and smiled, Samantha could not help but gaze into his beautiful brown eyes and think that he must have been drop dead gorgeous in his prime. Even now he was still quite handsome.

"I'm sorry, I'm being so rude - to both of you! Samantha Armstrong, I'm proud to introduce you to Upton Sheltra's newest partner, Kenny Tucker. Kenny Tucker, please meet my most important client from the Captive Services Division, Samantha Armstrong. Samantha is the President of Champlain Risk Systems."

Samantha became aware that she was still shaking Mr. Tucker's hand and he was laughing as he looked down at her. She could feel the color rising to her cheeks again, but she didn't let it bother her this time.

"Well, shall we?" he asked, pointing to the two chairs next to him.

Here Carlene took a deep breathe and began to tell another tale of woe, explaining why she had to run out on them both.

If he doesn't suggest it, I will, thought Samantha, just as Kenny said, "Well, I guess we're off the hook, Ms. Armstrong. Neither one of us can discuss business, so what do you say? Care to join me for a non-business lunch?"

"I'd love to" did manage to escape her lips before she plopped down in the chair closest to him and looked back up to see a stunned Carlene shaking her head. "Really Carlene, don't worry about it. Tell Tim to call me in a few days and we'll reschedule. You do what you have to do, we'll manage to entertain ourselves." Here she smiled at Kenny, who smiled back in return.

He dropped his head to look at the menu, but Samantha could not take her eyes off him. She reached for her menu and managed to open it (one of those albatrosses that are too big for the room, to say nothing about the table) without knocking anything over though.

"Well, congratulations. Partner. Must be the culmination of a lifetime of hard work and dedication. Your wife must be so proud." Did she really just say that? She wanted to die - how much more obvious could she be? She reached for the glass on the table in front of her and quickly drained it. It tasted a little funny. It wasn't water; it must be one of those new kinds of seltzer drinks on the market.

He laughed deeply. It had a good sound to it and was infectious.

"What? Not true?" she asked, while trying to have an innocent look on her face.

"Hmmm. Let's see. I'll have to break those statements apart to analyze."

"Wait a minute, I thought Carlene said you were a lawyer. You're not a psychiatrist too, are you? Because if my family sent you..." they both were still laughing and Samantha thought that this was the best few minutes she had ever had in her life.

"No. No. I'm a lawyer all right. It's just that you said 'life time', which makes me feel like an old man. And I don't want to feel like this is the end of something. I want this to be the beginning of something for me."

"Oh, me too," she said without thinking and cursed herself for acting so pathetic. This must be what people meant when they said that someone was acting like a lovesick schoolgirl! "I mean, of course you do. So what else about what I said bothered you?"

"Well I wouldn't exactly call what I have done hard work. I mean, there have been long hours and some difficult situations, but I've always been compensated quite nicely. You know there are times when I feel almost guilty, because I have been given so much for so little effort. It doesn't quite seem fair. Have you ever felt that your life has been some sort of mistake and pretty soon someone is going to find out and you're going to have to give back all your ill gotten gains?"

He was so adorable she couldn't stand it! She tried not to laugh at him, but his expression was so serious. This seltzer was delicious and seemed to have the magical power of regenerating itself automatically in her glass. She felt so absolutely wonderful and free right now. If only this lunch would never end. But as much as she wanted the fantasy to continue on one hand, she was dying to know where she stood on the other. She had to get him back to her original question about how his wife felt about all this.

"I can see I'm dining with a cynic here. You don't have any ill gotten gains?"

"Oh I'm sure I do, but I have no intention of returning them!"

He smiled again and lifted something on the side of the table. "Well I can see I've got a serious drinker on my hands. We're going to need another bottle of champagne," he said as he refilled their glasses with the bubbling liquid.

She almost dropped her glass. "You're kidding! I, I... don't drink!"

"Isn't that what they all say?"

"No really, I've never had a drink before in my life!"

"Oops. That MAY have been true before, but you're making up for lost time! Hey wait a minute. This isn't some sort of elaborate ruse to get me accused of sexual harassment, is it? Are we in a red light situation here?"

"Well I guess that all depends on how your wife feels about your promotion," she said before taking another sip. She was torn between the desire to stop drinking, yet also have something in front of her face to hide her disappointment, should the conversation take a turn.

"Oh, didn't I mention that I've never been married?"

"No you didn't."

"Well I haven't. Now, back to my question..."

"I would say that there are only green lights as far as the eye can see. Do you know that you are the easiest person to talk to? If you knew anything about me you would be shocked at my behavior right now. I don't think I've ever been more relaxed in my life. I hope you aren't planning to go back to work this afternoon."

"How can I, since your diabolical plan is to get me drunk and then take advantage of me!"

"In your dreams! You're the one preying on little ol' me. Little ol' innocent me, I might add. What kind of law firm are you running here?"

"If you keep mentioning business, I'm going to have to punish you. Let's get something straight. Kenny and Samantha are having a very nice luncheon date and we are not to discuss our jobs anymore. Deal?"

"That's going to be a little difficult for me, because all I've ever done is work. But you know what? I can't think of a single thing I want to tell you right now. All I want to do is hear everything there is to hear about you. I'm smitten Mr. Tucker. I don't mind telling you. If you don't watch yourself, I may decide to marry you someday."

"Forward little tramp, aren't you?"

They both collapsed into giggles as the waiter arrived to take their order.

"I haven't even looked at the menu yet!"

The waiter rolled his eyes before speaking through his teeth, "I can come back."

"Thanks-thanks a lot," Kenny said. Then turning to Samantha he said, "I'm not going to let that snotty kid ruin my day-so don't you either." They both laughed and then proceeded to talk about politics, religion, employee relations, his profession, hers-anything and everything they could think of. When the waiter returned for the fourth time, Kenny decided they had had enough. "You know what? Never mind. I told you to decide what you wanted when you first got here. But no, you had to spend all your time fooling around and not paying attention didn't you? I bet you aren't even hungry, are you, Samantha?"

"Not really." She tried to keep a straight face and play along with Kenny's game, but she could feel the anger welling up in the waiter behind her. Of course it probably wouldn't affect him too much that they were leaving without ordering. She had a feeling that Kenny was very generous in the tipping department. All that guilt about his ill gotten gains, no doubt.

"Let's leave," Kenny said as he stood shaking in his head in mock disgust. "Are you going to pay the bill, or what, you-you-hussy?"

Samantha and the waiter were both taken aback. She snatched the tab out of his hands, took a glance at the total, did a quick calculation in her head and then threw some bills down on the table.

"Sorry," she whimpered to the waiter and then ran to the elevator.

Kenny only joined her after walking very slowly across the room, with his head held high. Samantha burst out laughing as soon as they got inside the compartment. They were all alone. She grabbed him by the lapels, swung him around and pinned him against the back wall.

"Oh you're going to pay for that one, mister."

"Looking forward to it, Miss Armstrong. Please, God, at this point don't you dare tell me it is Mrs. Armstrong or I'm going to kill myself."

She stood on her tiptoes and kissed him gently on the mouth.

"I think I get to live..." he murmured softly in her ear as they descended to the parking garage.

Chapter 30

It wasn't until they reached the basement and the elevator doors opened to reveal a handful of their acquaintances that it occurred to them that they might want to be a little more discreet.

"Bill, Ron. How are you? Getting ready for the baseball season yet? How old are the kids now? Gosh, time flies, doesn't it?"

"Margie, hi. How's your sister-in-law? Good to see you, take care."

They both turned to go in opposite directions, since they were parked in different areas of the garage.

"I thought we'd take my car," he said, jingling his keys and pointing over his shoulder. "I've got a great idea for where we can go for some munchies to tide us over until tonight."

"I can meet you there, just tell me where."

"Nope," he said as he grabbed her by the hand and led her off towards his car. "I definitely like my idea better. I'm afraid if I let you out of my sight, I'm going to wake up from this dream and be devastated!"

"Well ok. I'd hate for that to happen. Just for the record though. Aren't we breaking every business and first date taboo here?"

"I think there are a few we have left intact. We're not related, are we?"

"I doubt it. You don't appear to be someone from the Northeast Kingdom."

"Oh my God! Don't tell me I've struck gold and caught myself a Real Vermonter?"

"The genuine article, but I'll never mention it again. Besides, I don't expect anyone is claiming me as such right now. I haven't exactly been very popular with my family in recent years and in the past few days, I've pretty much burned all those bridges."

He stopped dead in his tracks, as he sensed the change in her tone of voice. "Something tells me we've taken a serious turn here. Want to talk about it?"

"Not right now. Maybe when I've known you for five or six hours, I'll take you up on that offer." She tried to sound playful and bumped him at the hips.

"Here we are," he said and pointed with obvious pride at an immaculate dark green imported sports car.

"It's beautiful," she cooed as she walked around the back to take a complete look, "can I drive?"

She thought he was going to faint as all the color drained from his face. She braced herself in case his entire weight fell on her, but he quickly regained his composure.

"Do you really want to?" he asked incredulously. She could almost see the wheels spinning in his brain, could almost hear his inner voice yelling, "Noooooooooooo!"

She collapsed into a fit of laughter. "You really are too funny. I'm just kidding! Truth be told, I absolutely hate to drive. I never even got my license until I moved back to Vermont when I was in my late twenties!"

"Oh really? Interesting."

She wondered what the smirk on his face was for and then she smiled and said, "Yes, that's right. LAST YEAR when I moved back to

Vermont, I just knew I had to break down and get my license!"

He unlocked the passenger side and held the door for her. He was standing much too close to her and there was barely enough room for her to squeeze into the car, but she found the smell of him intoxicating. Or was that the champagne? Perhaps she was intoxicated?

What in God's name was she doing getting into a stranger's car in the middle of the day to go to some mystery location? What would her secretary say if she could see her now? The office! She hadn't even called in to let them know that the luncheon meeting had been cancelled and yet she wouldn't be returning to work this afternoon. What would her clients say? They would be appalled, that's for sure. But for once she was doing something just for herself, because she wanted to, and it felt good. Good and right. She hoped that they were headed to a mountaintop, because she felt like screaming, "I am in love!" at the top of her lungs.

"Hey, where did you say we were going?" she asked, as she shook herself from her daydream. They were long gone from downtown and heading out Williston Road.

"I feel like shooting some pool. Are you game?"

"Did someone give you a list of things I've never done before and challenge you to see how many you could introduce me to in a twenty four hour period or something?"

"Hmnn. Are you telling me I've got twenty four hours?"

"Well I'm afraid it's a pretty big list. Do you think twenty four hours is enough time to cover them all?"

"Give me some clues as to the rest of the items on this list. I thought later we could go to that fifties dance club down by the Lake. If you didn't mind indulging me with some real music, instead of what you probably listen to, that is."

"Since I am so young, that would be a terrible sacrifice on my part, but I think I could tolerate some oldies music. After all, it would cross another item off the list for me."

"Don't tell me you've never gone dancing!"

"BINGO! Oh yeah, that's something else I've never done!"

"What, played BINGO?"

"Yeah. How 'bout you?"

"You know what? Let's save that one for later. Maybe we both can cross that off our lists in about twenty years or so."

"Kind of optimistic, aren't you?"

"About what? Being around in twenty years?"

"Well that too, but I was referring to being with me." She raised her eyebrows and pretended to laugh while clapping her hands.

"Here it is!" he said as they pulled into a parking lot next to a large warehouse.

She reached for the handle, but he stretched across in front of her and locked the door. His elbow rubbed against her right breast and she could feel her nipple hardening underneath her bra. She held her breath as he kept his position for what seemed like an eternity. Her entire body was sending her brain signals it had never received before.

He finally turned in his seat and let his arm fall to her lap and then he touched her face gently with his other hand. He brushed her hair off her cheek and traced the outline of her ear. "Is it just me or do you feel it too?" he whispered as he bent to kiss her hard on the lips.

Her head was swimming, but she managed to sit upright in her seat, move his hand off her leg and say with a straight face, "you know I'm really looking forward to learning how to play pool. I hope you are going to be a good teacher."

"Don't worry. I'll be gentle," he said as he unlocked her door and jumped out the driver's side. In a flash he was around the car and opening her door.

She had a feeling he wasn't talking about a pool lesson. In fact, she was counting on it.

Chapter 31

Their destination wasn't anything like she had pictured; in fact, she was a little disappointed. Instead of the dark, smoky, crowded pool hall she imagined, they were standing in a bright, clear, clean, spacious club. The entire right hand side of the large building was filled with pool tables and as far as she could tell, the front section was a dance floor and the left-hand side had individual tables for various board games.

Kenny was apparently a regular. The man behind the counter greeted them warmly, extended his hand and exchanged a few personal pleasantries. "How about lucky number thirteen? Is that table free?"

"For you Kenny? Always. Follow me please," he waved them on, as he descended the three stairs from the bar to the table area. "I'll send Billy over, when he is finished taking the Trivial Pursuit orders. Hey, you interested in that tournament? There's a couple spots."

"Not today, Art. Thanks. Me & my special lady need some time alone - if you know what I mean. In fact, make sure you keep twelve and fourteen clear, ok?" At this point he slipped Art a hundred-dollar bill.

Samantha leaned against the pool table and started rolling the balls around with her hands. Kenny came up behind her and again was too close for comfort. His smell overwhelmed her and she had to close her eyes and take a deep breath. Suddenly she didn't feel very well, her stomach was killing her. Food! They hadn't eaten and she was starving.

"Hey, would it be terribly rude of me to insist that we eat before we start this lesson," she said without turning around to face him. She was afraid to do that for fear that she wouldn't be able to control herself. In her mind's eye they were kissing passionately as she ripped the clothes from his body.

The fantasy was interrupted by his question, "What do you want, anyway?" She realized with a giggle that he wasn't saying that in the middle of their illicit tryst, he had in fact said that while looking at the menu that Billy brought.

"I'll keep it simple, bring me one of everything-I'm famished!"

"Well you heard the lady, Billy. Bring on the whole enchilada. And Billy? Don't be a hero, man." Kenny's laughter was greeted with confusion by Samantha... it didn't clear anything up for her when the waiter called back over his shoulder as he headed into the kitchen, "You know that was funny the first 1,000 times you said it, guy. Right now it's gettin' a little old though. Kinda like you, now that I think about it!"

"Hey that's funny. Remind me when I'm paying the bill how funny you are, Ok?"

"Do I even want to know what that was all about?" asked Samantha, when Kenny stopped laughing and turned back to her.

"I love that one, don't you? It's a classic. They just never tire."

"I don't get it."

"Come on. Billy, don't be a hero? Don't be a fool with your li-i-ife." He was singing at this point and doing a little dance.

"What in God's name are you talking about?" she managed to get out before collapsing in laughter. Kenny kept singing, then grabbed her and started to dance around the pool table. The song was too emotional though and required his full concentration, so he just held her hand while writhing to the rest of the verse and chorus.

"Oh man, it's going to be a long day with you two, isn't it?" asked Billy, when he returned with drinks that as far as Samantha could tell, they hadn't ordered. "I took the liberty of bringing your usual, Kenny. What can I get you, ma'am?"

"Well for starters, you can get me a hand to slap you silly - if you're going to call me ma'am, I'm going to feel as ancient as this clown."

"Sorry - it was meant as a term of respect, but I should know by now that you northerners find that offensive!"

"I'm sorry, it's just the way I've been acting today. I think this clown is responsible! I don't feel it necessary for you to respect me. Wait, that didn't come out right. Never mind, I'll just take a glass of water, if that won't be too much trouble."

"OOOO. Water. That's exciting. I don't think so my dear. The night is young and so are - well, dammit - so are you! She'll have some champagne, Billy. And keep it coming, she's a real lush."

"Hey! Don't be a fool with your li-i-ife." She fell against him and they both kept laughing, while Billy just shook his head and went in the direction of the bar. "You know, I'm really going to regret this in the morning, but right now I must say I am having the time of my life. Who would have guessed this possible? If anyone I work with sees me like this, I'm ruined. All these years of building up this reputation as a cold and unfeeling witch - wasted. For what? A fling with Grandpa?"

"I don't mind saying I'm starting to realize where the cold and unfeeling part comes from. If you make one more crack about my age, I'm going to have to teach you a lesson!"

"Yeah, promises, promises old man." She quickly gave him a light kiss on the cheek and then ran to the table that someone was filling up with appetizers. "Hot! Hot!" she screamed as her fingers were singed on the temptations before her.

"My thoughts exactly," he whispered in her ear as he swung onto the stool beside her. "I hope you're hungry, because you ordered enough for fifty people!"

"Well I have a few friends dropping over shortly, so I wanted to be prepared." She winked when he pouted at the thought of visitors intruding on their fun.

They took a break in the conversation to work on devouring everything before them. It was then that Samantha wondered why her nipples hurt. Casually looking down at her shirt, she was shocked to see that they were huge. Practically jumping through her blouse. She noticed Kenny looking at them too.

"Hey... don't eat everything while I'm gone... I've got to visit the ladies room." She fumbled for a few seconds trying to get up, since the stools were secured to the floor and she was trying to push hers away from the counter. He wiped his hands and mouth on a napkin and then stood up to assist her.

"Thank you. You've got a little bit of sauce in the corner - yeah, right there. Your tongue got it. Yup. Right there. Uh, I'll be back," she stammered as she hurried in the direction of the dance floor, hoping the bathrooms were somewhere close by. Her face felt flushed again and she couldn't get the image of his tongue circling his mouth to find the offending morsel, out of her mind. Where was this heading? Was she setting herself up for a fall? She was certainly falling for this man. This wonderfully funny, handsome, older, sophisticated, insane man.

She took in her reflection in the mirror as she entered the powder room and couldn't believe her eyes. Her hair was wildly framing her face, her eyes were so bright and the smile on her face was so foreign she had to reach out and touch it on the glass. She was most certainly drunk, she realized this. But it didn't change anything. After relieving the pressure in her bladder, she felt much better as she straightened her blouse and skirt. Boldly, she unbuttoned her top button and did a few turns for the mirror while holding her hair in various positions and pretending to laugh silently to survey how it looked.

She jumped a few inches in the air and let out a yelp when the sound of the door opening brought her back to reality. A few coughs for good measure - one more look at the new Samantha and then back to her fella. Did she actually just think of Kenny as her fella? Oh my God, what was coming next on the agenda?

She said a silent prayer just before she returned, hoping she wasn't making a fool out of herself. "So what if I am," she thought as she covered Kenny's eyes and whispered, "Guess who?" with a Southern accent.

"Billy, is that you?" said Kenny in mock surprise.

"Ok, feeding time is over. I'm ready for that lesson now. Remember, you promised to go easy on me," she said as she leaned over his shoulder and looked into his eyes.

"I'm rethinking that one now. You may be an advanced student. I'm going to bend a few rules and rush right to the complicated stuff. Watch and learn my friend."

He took two pool cues off the rack and handed Samantha one. Then he bent to work organizing the balls for the break.

*

Two hours later they finished their last game and were headed to the dance club. She couldn't wait to be alone with him in the car. Maybe she'd get lucky and he'd brush up against her again. Or maybe he'd get lucky and she would just out and out attack him! Either way, she was going to take this night to the next level. Hopefully she'd be able to cross something else off her list very shortly!

Chapter 32

"Pardon me for being impertinent, but isn't there a dance floor in this building we are currently leaving?" she managed to ask between giggles as she carefully walked down the handicapped ramp to Kenny's car.

"My darling, did you hear any music?"

"Well as a matter of fact I did, but I think it was only in my head!"

They both laughed at this as he fumbled with his keys trying to open the passenger side door for Samantha. She suspected that the difficulty was not caused because he was drunk, but rather that he was having trouble functioning with her hot breathe on the back of his neck. Finally the key slid into the lock and he was holding the door open and reaching for her hand to help ease her into the vehicle.

Once seated she rearranged her skirt, blouse and hair again. The minute his door slammed, she could feel the color rising to her cheeks. What was it about being so close to him? Her whole body was tingling and she knew it was more than an alcoholic buzz.

"ANYWAY," he announced as the car shot out onto Williston Road between oncoming cars in both directions, "I was explaining about the dance floor."

"Oh yes, please continue," she faced his direction and then bowed her head toward the floorboards, while moving her hands in a mock form of worship.

"The establishment we just left is my favorite pool haunt, but their DJ doesn't start until much later in the evening and..." he pursed his lips here, "how shall I say? It is not their forte!?!?!"

"Well you shouldn't go to a lot of trouble for me."

He smiled during a long, thoughtful look in her direction and then finally said with a wink, "I think we both know you're worth a little trouble."

She could feel the burn rising to her cheeks again, so she returned the smile quickly and then turned toward the window and pretended to be engrossed in the view. They were at their next stop within ten minutes. The place was practically empty, but the music was pounding and the drinks were flowing. Between dancing every dance and continuing to absorb the champagne that Kenny kept supplying, she was exhausted. During the fast numbers he talked about his work. When it was slowed down and they embraced, Samantha told him about her world. At some point, she simply passed out.

* *

Kenny's arms enveloped her and their bodies started to sway to the music. She was aware of clouds swirling around their legs, as they moved to the music coming from the harpsichords played by the angels floating by. Their wings were moving very fast and she could feel the breeze that was generated against her face.

Somewhere in the distance she heard her name being called. Instantaneously it went from a bright sunny day to a cold, dark night. The angels abruptly stopped playing and fled the area with fearful looks shot back in the direction of the voice. Samantha squinted in the blackness, trying to define the figure that was approaching. Kenny had vanished into thin air. She brought her knees in close to her chest and hugged herself tightly, trying to stop from shivering. Her body bobbed up and down in the night air, as if she were sailing on the high seas.

"Hello Sam," her mother said, as she reached out to brush stray hairs out of her eyes, "It's good to see you finally happy."

Samantha started to smile, but then she noticed that her mother's face did not mirror her look of joy.

"Hi Mommy," she managed to choke out before the tears started to gush from her eyes, "what are you doing here?"

"You need to know the truth, baby. I left you a note, but you haven't read it yet. Don't you want to know the truth?" Her mother extended her hand and Samantha could see the yellowed envelope that her Grandmother had given her the day of her father's funeral.

She tentatively reached out toward her mother, but a sound in the distance made her stop for a moment. It was laughter. She knew it was her Grandmother, before she came into view. She flew towards them cackling. Samantha made a lunge toward the envelope, but it was too late. Her Grandmother snatched it away and disappeared into the blackness. Samantha touched her mother's hand, but the flesh melted away and only a skeleton remained, and even that quickly turned to dust in her fingers. She was alone again, but she could hear another voice coming from where the others had originated. Was it her father this time? Her Grandfather? No. It was Kenny.

She awoke with a violent shudder. It was just a dream. A nightmare. She was back in Kenny's car.

Her blouse was soaked by the combination of the tears streaming down her face and the fact that her body temperature had gone through the roof. She was concentrating on getting her breathing under control, until she realized the look of horror on Kenny's face.

"Are you alright, Samantha? I thought I was losing you there for a minute. You really scared me. Are you OK?" His face was contorted, as he checked that all her limbs were still intact.

"Oh Kenny, I am so sorry. I must have fallen asleep, but then I had this feeling that my mother was... Oh, whew. I'm sorry and SO embarrassed. Could I... I mean, could you just bring me back to my car? I think I need to go home and collect myself."

"Whoa, slow down. Don't you want to tell me about it?"

"No. Not now. Thanks anyway, but I'm not sure what is going on. I've ruined your evening, so I'd just feel better if I was by myself. I'm sorry."

"Listen. I have no problem with taking you home, but there is no way that I am going to leave you alone or let you drive a car right now. You haven't ruined anything for me, but I'm afraid that I've done something terribly wrong to you."

He started the car and she was able to take a minute to look around and get her bearings. It was still fairly early, so she could tell that they were close to the waterfront. She didn't have the strength to argue about her car and oddly enough, the last thing she wanted to do was drive home alone.

It took a few minutes for her to realize that although the car was running, they weren't going anywhere yet. She turned to look at Kenny, who was drumming the steering wheel with his fingers and staring intently straight ahead.

"Thanks," she said quietly, as she reached out to touch his arm.

He turned, smiled and then sheepishly asked, "Could you give me a hint where you live?"

They both laughed and some of the tension eased between them. She gave the simplest instructions, even though it wasn't the quickest way to her house. This time, she sat bolt upright. There was no way she would allow herself to doze off again.

Chapter 33

"I must say I am impressed," Kenny said after a whistle, as they pulled into her driveway. "What a perfect location... and the house! I can't wait to see how it is set up. Well... I mean - I'd like to walk you inside and make sure that you are really ok before I leave... so naturally, while inside I would have the chance to see - Oh to Hell with it! Are you going to let me babble on like this forever or are you going to put me out of my misery???"

Samantha smiled. "I can't thank you enough. I have no idea what to say to explain myself. I feel like everything I have ever known about who I was and what my life was all about was taken from me about a week ago and I'm working without a road map here. I know that can't possibly make any sense to you, but yet here you are making me feel like I'm going to be alright."

"Hey - let's get you inside. No offense, but I think you need to take a long, hot shower and change your clothes. That must have been some nightmare."

"Well thank you. I will take that advice and I'm sure I will feel 100% better afterwards. You don't need to walk me in - I'm perfectly fine now. Really."

"Nice try little lady, but you can't get rid of me that easy. Have no fear, I'll let you know when it's time for me to leave."

Have no fear. That was a reasonable expectation for her, but she couldn't shake the feeling of her chest being squeezed by a vice. So much so that she found it difficult to breathe without concentrating on it. She couldn't fool herself into thinking that being alone was desirable at this point. She simply smiled and nodded slightly in Kenny's direction. Again he was out of the car in a flash and then right beside her once more, assisting her out of the vehicle.

Suddenly she realized how cold it was, with the clammy clothing pasted to her skin. She brushed the damp hair away from her forehead and out of her eyes, just as they reached the back entrance. The minute inside she kicked off her shoes, threw her coat in the corner and headed for the bathroom.

"You don't lock your door?" he asked somewhat irritated.

"Sorry. It's the woodchuck in me." She had to laugh at the confused look on his face. "I'm sorry, I thought all you Flatlanders called us Vermonters woodchucks - NO?"

"Oh that! I'm glad you cleared that up because I was about to start looking through the house for some sort of elaborate cage system. Didn't know if perhaps it was a vampire/werewolf thing and you were in the midst of transforming or something."

She didn't feel like laughing anymore, but it wasn't a bad thing. She was more comfortable with this man than any other human being she had encountered and she wanted to know more about him.

"Well, if you don't mind, I'm going to take that shower now. But I would really like it if you would stick around."

"Pretty please?"

"Pretty please with a cherry on top?"

"Well if you're going to give me a cherry, than that settles it. I'm not going anywhere. Take your time. I'll be here when you get out."

She mouthed thank you from the end of the hall and he gave her a little salute. After shedding the rest of her clothes and starting the shower, she realized that she hadn't told him to help himself to anything or to make himself comfortable. But she wasn't worried. He would quickly find his way around and everything would be ok. Better than ok, in fact. She had a feeling that things were going to be better than ever.

Chapter 34

By the time the hot water had magically transformed her body and soul, she was embarrassed at the thought of not having a stitch of clothing to change into - or a towel large enough to cover her completely if she were to attempt a dash to her bedroom. So towels don't actually wash themselves and get restocked during the day while I am at work? It was the first time she had thought of Jeannie in quite a while. What a pair they had been - users, both of them. They had deserved each other...

There was a soft knock on the door. "Hey - are you ok in there?"

"Well yes and no. I feel much better, thank you, but I'm afraid I don't have enough thread in here with me to sew some sort of coverall!"

"Hmmm. Interesting! Well let me in and I'll see what I can throw together!"

"Don't you dare!" she screamed.

"Ok, ok. I must confess that I've been kind of nosing around and I do in fact have a robe in my hand right now. I think it might belong to you, so why don't you reach out and give it a try?"

"Are you serious?"

"Yes, I am. Here you go. Oops. Where are you? I'm holding it out, but you aren't taking it," he said as he kept the robe from meeting her wildly groping hand.

"Very funny, wise guy. Just give me the damn robe!"

"Ooooo - feisty when we are wet and naked, aren't we?"

"Pardon me, but who said I was wet or naked?"

"Believe me, I can tell - Here you go!" He tossed the robe towards her, but it landed half in, half out of the doorway.

"Ok. Enough fun and games. I've made coffee, get your butt out here, because we've got a lot of ground to cover tonight!"

"What are you talking about?" she asked while slipping into the warm, soft robe that had already picked up the incredible scent of him. After inhaling long and hard, she realized that he had said something. She opened the door and cocked her ear to listen because he had returned to the kitchen. She could hear the clinking of glassware and soft humming. Was he doing the dishes? "What?" she called. No response.

She checked her reflection in the mirror - shook her head and padded out to the kitchen, cinching the robe tight around her middle.

Without turning around or lifting his head from his work he asked, "Don't you ever do dishes? I'm not sure if you are aware of this or not, but see that square door over there to the right? You can actually pull that handle down and inside is the wonderful, new fangled machine called - are you ready for this? - a dishwasher! It's true! I kid you not!"

"Ha, ha, very funny. Message received."

"You see, when you have dirty dishes you simply put them inside, add a little soap from under the sink here, lock the handle, turn the other knob on the front and then presto, chango, they are CLEANED! Of course the bad news is that you then have to open the special box back up, take the dishes out and then put them away. So it isn't as magical as it could be!"

"Oh yeah, you're a laugh riot. Come here," she said as she turned him away from the sink, where he was still hard at work. When she saw that he was wearing one of Jeannie's aprons around his waist, she couldn't contain her laughter.

"What? What is it?" he asked with his wet, soapy hands held out to his sides.

His serious expression softened just as she asked, "I'm a little confused. If this little machine that I apparently have is so wondrous, why are you doing the dishes by hand?"

She screamed in surprise as he scooped her up in his arms and carried her into the living room. "Oh I never could use the things myself. Our housekeeper always washed the dishes thoroughly first and then put them in the dishwasher. I could never see the point of that. Seemed like twice the work to me. So I always wash them by hand."

"I think you're a grown up boy now and capable of making your own decisions. I won't tell your housekeeper if you cheat and put them in without rinsing!"

"What can I say? She's scarred me for life. I'd never be able to do that for fear of dropping dead on the spot! Besides-you want to hear something really scary? I actually enjoy washing dishes. But only in a kitchen like yours. One with a window over the sink. Don't know why, but it makes me happy."

"What was that you were singing?"

"Was I singing something? I didn't realize."

"Yeah, when I was coming up the hall it sounded like..."

"Listen. You are stalling. I've got our coffee ready and we can stay up all night talking if we have to. And believe me, that is not something I say every day. In fact, I have never before said it-I can't believe I'm saying it now and I hope I never say it again as long as I live!"

She took the coffee cup he handed her and closed her eyes as the strong liquid warmed her insides to match the outside. Sitting in her house with this man, she wanted to talk. For the first time in her life she wanted to tell someone else about her Mother, her Father, the letter, everything. So she did...

Chapter 35

"I don't understand - read it already!"

"After everything I just told you, how can you say that?"

"So don't read it... throw it away!"

"Are you crazy? You're not helping!"

"I'm sorry babe, but the truth is it's your decision to make and only you can decide. If you want to read your Mom's letter, then do it. But do it right now and be done with it. If you don't want to, then throw it away-right now-and never think about it again. It's as simple as that!"

"First of all, it's more complicated than that—"

"Only because you are making it that way."

"Please don't interrupt me - and second of all, did you call me babe?"

"I'll interrupt you whenever I damn well please and yes, I called you that, is there a problem - babe?"

"The only problem I have is that I can't decide what to do and it is haunting me. Babe is fine, actually, I was just checking. Should I call you some cutesy name or something more formal? Kenneth, perhaps?"

"I'm not much on cutesy for myself. Anyway, Kenny is my real name. Hey! Stop changing the subject."

"It's not short for anything?"

"Did I not just say that?"

"Well what's the deal with that?"

"You know what? Let's agree to solve one mystery at a time, ok? Ok?"

"Do you know what time it is?"

"Yes I am aware of the time, but I couldn't care less. I've got a couple good hours left in me, but I'd rather spend them doing something besides rehashing the same old arguments."

"Will you at least acknowledge the fact that I can't make this decision lightly because the contents of that letter are going to affect me for the rest of my life?"

"Why?"

"Why? How can it not affect me? I have no idea what's inside."

"Exactly. You have no idea. Until a week ago you didn't even know a letter existed and THAT had been influencing you your entire life, whether you realized it or not. Listen to me." He took her shoulders and gently turned her body, so that they were facing each other. "What possible difference could it make, no matter what it says?"

The break in the banter going quickly back and forth made Samantha uncomfortable. Staring at the floor, kicking at the carpet with her toes, she retightened her robe and tucked her arms underneath her chest so she was no longer exposing herself.

Kenny reached up slowly with his finger under her chin and lifted her face towards his. "What is it really? What are you afraid of?"

"What... what if it... what if she blames me - you know, for it all?" she said barely above a whisper, with the tears choking in her throat.

Kenny smiled and Samantha could see the tears starting to form in his eyes as well. "I just met you how many hours ago? Maybe I'm wrong-tell me if I am-but what difference would it/SHOULD IT make in your life today, IF that's what the letter says?"

She reached up to wipe some of the tears away as they streamed down her cheeks. It was too late to stop the onslaught. "Don't you think knowing that could kill a person?"

"No. No I don't. And how do I know that? Because that's what you've believed all your life anyway. Isn't it?" he questioned. "That the drinking, your Mother's suicide, your Father's leaving-everything, it was all your fault?"

She tried to get off the couch before the sobs wracked her body, but he held firm. Kenny didn't pull her towards him; he simply did not let her move further away. After a few seconds she sat back down and slowly put her arms around him. She cried on his shoulder and in his neck, like she had never cried before. He stroked her hair and hugged her to him all the time saying, "It will be alright, baby. I promise you it will be alright."

And she believed him...

Chapter 36

As far as she could tell, there hadn't been a dream or a nightmare. When she awoke the sun was shining in her face, her back was killing her for having slept on the couch, but her head was clear and she was otherwise all right.

More glassware was clinking in the kitchen. Was he taking the dishes out of the cupboards to wash? She could tell that he was humming again. She quietly went to the doorway to listen, so she would be able to identify the song this time. It was a sad song, she knew that, but she couldn't place it. He wasn't humming it right, that was what was confusing her. His tempo was too upbeat for the lyrics.

Soapsuds splashed everywhere as he jumped, when he heard her behind him.

"I'm sorry, I didn't mean to startle you."

He smiled and grabbed at his chest, "Whew! Remember my old heart the next time you want to sneak up on me," he said.

"I wasn't sneaking," she said indignantly, "besides, it's my house!"

His mood shifted as he let the water out of the sink and used the hose to spray the soap scum off the sides of it. "I'm a - I feel terrible about this, but I've got to run this morning" he spat out as he untied Jeannie's apron, threw it on the kitchen table and bent to give her a quick kiss on the cheek.

She knew the smile had faded from her lips and now the cloud that had been hanging over her for days returned. But this time it seemed darker and weighed more heavily on her heart.

Oh God, she thought, he's going to make up some excuse for leaving and I will never see him again! I've poured out my inner most thoughts and fears to this man, this STRANGER, and now he thinks I'm as crazy as a loon and he's going to run away as fast as he can. She was about to ask him if something was wrong, when she heard a noise in the garage. "What the hell is that?" she questioned, heading towards the door.

"Just a minute," he said, as he reached out to stop her with his hands still wet from the dishes, "I know this is short notice, but I need to drive to Boston on Saturday and I would love it if you would come along."

A little bit of life returned to her body and she said, "Sure. I'd like that too."

He looked at the floor and said quickly, "My Mom is in a nursing home there. I don't expect you to come in with me, of course, but I thought we could head down to the Cape after and spend the night. I mean, if that's something that interests you."

"Yes, I am interested. Thank you for asking." She wanted to throw her arms around him and whisper, Yes, Yes, my darling in his ear, but she settled for a quick hug instead. "Hey, is that a dagger in your pocket or are you just happy to see me?" she asked when something in his pants poked her. She giggled at her stupid joke-not noticing that Kenny's face turned bright red. A noise outside broke her mood. She didn't notice as he secretively took out a box and moved it to his overcoat. Right as she reached for the door handle, it turned and Jeannie burst into the room. Samantha jumped back, startled.

"Well, well, well," Jeannie clucked, as she took in the sight of Kenny and Samantha's attire. "It looks like someone took my advice after all! So how was it? Must have been something after saving yourself up all these years! Lucky you didn't burst into flames!" She laughed nervously; hoping that Samantha would join in with her and everything would be back to the way it had been only a few short days before. But that wasn't going to happen.

"What do you want?" Samantha asked through clenched teeth, while Kenny collected his scattered belongings - tie, socks, shoes and a belt. When Jeannie didn't immediately answer, she added, "I'll take my key, thank you very much!" and snatched the item out of Jeannie's hand before she could respond.

"So Mr. Tucker," Jeannie said sarcastically, as Kenny tried to go around her and make his way out the door awkwardly, "how are tricks?"

"You two know each other?" Samantha asked, suddenly nervous that her fragile universe was about to take another hit. She slumped down in a chair to better steady herself for what was about to come. She prayed silently, repeating over and over again, "Anything, God, anything except that they've slept together. I couldn't take that!"

"Yes, I know Mr. Tucker," Jeannie continued, "My friend Diane has a sister - Ginger isn't it, Ken?"

"Whatever Jeannie, I really don't care," she said. "Nothing has changed, you have no reason for being here and I want you out!" Was it her imagination, or did the color return to Kenny's face?

Kenny interrupted with, "I'll call you at work this afternoon, Ok Samantha?" he looked to her for reassurance and then he turned to

Jeannie and said, "Nice seeing you again. I trust that you'll take care." The way he said it suggested that it was not nice seeing her again and he was threatening her to be careful. Or warning her?

"Well. I guess it was a waste of time coming here. I'll walk out with you then." Jeannie turned abruptly and followed closely at Kenny's heels. Samantha leaned against the door and waved to Kenny questioningly as he left through the garage and then closed the door slowly behind her.

She thought she heard voices out in the driveway, so she went to the front window where she could clearly see Kenny and Jeannie yelling at each other and gesturing wildly. She strained to catch the words, but it was all a jumble of sounds. What is going on, she thought and then ran back to the door determined to find out. By the time she reached the driveway, however, all that remained was the sight of the two cars speeding up the road.

Another mystery, she thought disgustedly, as she headed back into the empty garage. Her car! It was still in the underground lot where she had left it last night with a few drops of gas in it. How was she going to get to work? What was she going to do at work, once she got there? She would need to spend the morning making up for all that she had missed yesterday afternoon. She knew the afternoon would be spent thinking about the envelope or what the connection between Kenny and Jeannie was. She decided against both. She would simply ask Kenny what his relationship with Jeannie was and that would be the end of that. As to the other, she vowed that moment to open the envelope when they returned from the Cape. One way or another, she would have some answers on Monday. What a way to start a new week!

Chapter 37

She took her time getting ready and then didn't fret when the taxi was 20 minutes late. She just smiled when the driver greeted her with, "You didn't call and ask why I wasn't here, did you?"

As they were approaching her office, she changed her mind, "You know what? I'm sorry, but I just realized this is crazy. My car is downtown in the Courthouse Mall parking garage, so I might as well pick it up now, instead of having to get another ride over there later."

He seemed irritated until she passed a fifty-dollar bill across the seat and said, "For your trouble, of course."

"You're calling the shots, lady" he called over his shoulder as he quickly changed lanes, offending two or three other drivers in the process.

That I am thought Samantha, as she sat back against the seat and relaxed until they arrived at the underground garage. She thanked the cab driver, who in turn enthusiastically thanked her for her business and requested that she call him again anytime. Then she waved to the parking attendant as she walked by his booth. She didn't let the smirk on his face affect her mood when she presented her ticket from the previous afternoon. She smiled and said, "Hey, at least I'm wearing a change of clothes!"

It was lucky for her that the gas station was about 100 yards from the exit, as her car would not have made it much further. She gassed up, took in the sun and clouds and lovely sights and sounds of Burlington and then headed back up Shelburne Road to CRS.

As she suspected, things were in quite a state of turmoil when she arrived. There were a million questions, but she managed to get everyone back on track to normal operations (whatever normal meant anymore) within forty-five minutes of her entrance. She threw herself into her work and felt incredible by the time three o'clock rolled around. She hadn't thought about any of the things that could have brought her mood down. She refused to. What had the cabby said? She was calling the shots? Damn straight, she thought. I'm going to have one hell of a weekend, I'd bet my life on it. Better watch out, Kenny, 'cause here I come!

Chapter 38

Kenny had a problem arise with a client, so leaving for Boston on Friday night wasn't an option. Even though Samantha was a little disappointed that she wouldn't see him for another day, she was also somewhat relieved that she had an additional night to pack.

She had no idea what to bring for clothing, as she had a hard time imagining how romance would fit in with a weekend visit to your Mother in an old age home! Kenny isn't exactly a spring chicken - how old is this poor woman? On her deathbed?

After spending what seemed like hours in front of her closet slamming every outfit she owned, she finally decided it was time to enlist some help from someone who would know what to do. She headed to the Mall and decided to get the hardest (and most humiliating) part out of the way first. No since spending all her time and money on accessories and then have the stores close before she could get a piece de la resistance for the grand finale. She didn't like the sound of that! Making love with Kenny should be the start of something, not the end of something else.

All her insecurities and inhibitions were sucked inside her as she sheepishly looked around for any familiar faces and then ducked into the Victoria's Secret show room. She had already walked by at least ten times, waiting until the saleswoman she had picked out to approach was in the back corner of the store.

Samantha marched determinedly by older husbands holding their wives' pocketbooks; young anorexic, half-dressed ghosts who were trying to decide which of three styles of underwear to buy. They all looked the same to her and also seemed to be sizes that would have been too small for Samantha to wear-even at birth!

Just as she reached her destination, a dressing room door flew open and a woman about her age and build emerged wearing an outfit that Samantha would have been uncomfortable with in the privacy of her own home. What am I doing here, she thought, and turned quickly to leave before she made an even bigger fool out of herself.

Whether the saleswoman was moved by the initial look of determination or the thought of a possible high commission sale, she would never know; however, she deftly stepped in front of her and purred, "How can I help you tonight?"

Samantha was speechless for a moment, unsure whether she really wanted to leave or not. Finally that new found inner voice that kept telling her to take a chance with Kenny won out and she quietly whispered, "I'm-a-going away for the weekend with a gentleman and I've never done THAT before, if you know what I mean!" Whether the woman had any idea what she was talking about or not, she did not falter. She reached out, leading her gently to a chair in the back corner, after mumbling something about taking care of everything, she went from one end of the store to the other furiously looking through racks and shelves, grabbing every fifth item or so.

Samantha enjoyed watching as she talked to herself, shook her head in disgust with poor choices or nodded enthusiastically when she was pleased with her selection. In a few minutes she was back covered with clothing thrown over each shoulder and hangers dangling from almost every finger.

"I think these might be what you had in mind," she questioned as she proceeded to display her from sunup to sundown collection. There was a little black dress that would be perfect for the car ride down. If Kenny changed his mind about her meeting his Mom, it looked sexy and smart, not trashy and dumb. There was a fire engine red lacy bra and matching panties. A skimpy black teddy and a long, sheer robe. One more daytime outfit, black slacks with a teal/black top. Again, sexy yet sharp. Good for brunch alone with Kenny or with his Mother. She loved them all and they were even her size! Considering that even she would have had to ask Jeannie what that was a few short days ago, she was particularly impressed. She didn't want to ask what the other items were-no matter, since they seemed to have too many hooks and wires and not enough material. She held up one of the contraptions and honestly could not tell what it was supposed to be or how in God's name you wore it.

"How did you do that? I'm stunned. I just said one sentence and you picked out all these things that are just what I wanted and they are my size and I'm going to take them. How did you know?"

The woman smiled. "You are really good at your job, aren't you?"

Samantha was somewhat taken aback, "Well, yes as a matter of fact, I am. I would say that I'm the best at what I do."

"Me too," she winked, "just so happens that not everyone is as appreciative or impressed as you appear to be."

"Well they should be! Thank you so much. As I'm sure you could tell, I was a nervous wreck, but now I'm feeling pretty good about everything."

"Don't you want to try everything on?" she asked as she pointed toward an open dressing room.

"Oh my God, I couldn't!" Samantha was slightly hurt that the woman found this amusing.

"Sure you can - come on, I'll help you."

"No, no, no. Thanks anyway. I'm all set. I'm going to take these things. Uh, those other things" she waved her hand at the mystery pieces that intrigued her, but not enough to get in a room the size of a closet with a Jane Doe, "I'm going to pass on this time, but hey, I may be back!"

"Anytime. I'll look forward to it," she said as she gathered the clothing up and brought Samantha to a register in the middle of the store, "except Mondays."

When Samantha looked at her questioningly, she smiled, "That's my day off," she giggled.

"Well if this weekend goes as fantastic as I'm hoping, I'll see you on Tuesday," she called over her shoulder as she left with her purchases. And maybe I'll even be ready to experiment with some of those other things, she thought happily as she began to hum a tune. It was that song she had heard Kenny hum in her kitchen. Kenny. She gave herself a little squeeze and picked up the pace. The sooner she got home to pack, the better. She couldn't wait for tomorrow.

Chapter 39

As it turned out, she shouldn't have been in such a rush to get home. Once there, she packed and repacked her overnight case a dozen times and tried on every outfit at least five times. She played and replayed scenario after scenario in her head, trying to prepare herself for every possible sexual encounter.

Would they give in to their passion in the car, when they arrived at the bed and breakfast on the Cape? No, she did not want her first time to be in a parking lot, where curious on lookers could join in and ruin her moment.

When they checked in to the room, would he come up behind her while she was unpacking and gently run his big, beautiful hands all over her body before slipping off her new black dress? She made a mental note to wear the new bra and underwear set underneath, just in case.

Or would they be able to restrain themselves through a nice candlelit dinner? After dessert and coffee would they stroll hand in hand upstairs, so that she could whisper, "I'll be right back, I want to slip into something more comfortable" in his ear? She imagined herself coming out of the bathroom wearing the black teddy. She could picture the look on his face, feel the touch of his hands and take in the wonderful smell of him. But in all of these images he was either fully dressed, or in a bed completely covered with a comforter.

She tried to envision her reaction to seeing his body for the first time. She had spent a lot of time hoping that she wouldn't disappoint him; it hadn't occurred to her that she might be the one to end up disappointed. I don't think that is possible, she thought, I'm just so happy when I am with him. And even now, just thinking about him brings a smile to my face.

What about birth control? Would he take care of, should she? She slapped herself in the forehead as she went into the bathroom and took her birth control pills out of the medicine chest. What an idiot I am, she thought as she put them in her purse. She had been taking the pill since college, when her doctor had recommended it for regulating her cycle. Before that she had suffered debilitating periods, where she would be forced to spend at least one day each month in bed or in the bathroom doubled over in pain. That seemed so long ago. She hardly gave her monthly "friend" (as her Grandmother always called it) a thought these days. And it certainly had been awhile since she had connected her "medicine" with the idea of birth control.

Her Grandmother had forbidden her to take the pill in high school when it was first suggested, so Samantha had waited until College and then done it without her consent. She understood why the thought made her nervous. After all Nanny, she thought, here I am almost 40 years old and jumping in bed with the first guy that shows any interest in me. Did taking the pill make me a slut, or what?

She gasped as she noted by the bedside clock that it was three o'clock in the morning. That's it. Time to pack it in and get some sleep. She crawled between the covers and fell into oblivion almost immediately. When the alarm went off, she was momentarily annoyed, before she remembered what day it was and jumped out of bed. A cup of strong coffee, half a bagel and a quick shower set the wheels in motion. She had just finished her hair and makeup when she heard Kenny knock on the door before coming in.

"You look incredible!" he said when she met him in the kitchen with her bags. "God I've missed you." He gave her a kiss on the cheek and a full body hug. "Come on. I've got so much to tell you. It's been quite a week."

"Ready when you are," she said as they left. This bra is killing me, she thought, as she hooked her seat belt and smiled at Kenny as he slipped in beside her. Oh I'm going to be feeling real sexy by the time we get to Boston! I may have to rip it off myself! Now won't that make for an interesting car trip!

Chapter 40

"Okay Mr. Tucker. I have you all to myself for the next few hours and I want to hear everything about you. Start from the beginning and don't leave a thing out. My life has been an open book to you, but you are practically a mystery man to me. Don't forget to slip in there somewhere why your real name is Kenny, not Kenneth, either!" She said as they turned onto Shelburne Road and headed for the Interstate.

"You know that I would love to tell you my life story (and I will), but first I've got to tell you something else. It is very important and I should have told you the minute I met you, but I didn't and now, I just want to do it before it gets forgotten and comes up later to screw something up for us." He looked positively frightened and he was gripping the steering wheel so hard that his knuckles were white.

"Oh God, don't tell me you lied about being married!" she screamed as her hands went to her face in horror.

"No. It's not that. I never lied to you. Not about being married. I was engaged though - well I was going to ask a woman to marry me, but then I changed my mind. But she heard about it because a friend of hers worked in the jewelry store where I bought the ring. So it was real awkward and there was a big fight. I knew all along that I shouldn't marry her because I didn't love her. But after awhile you think that you can settle. That you should settle, because maybe no one better is ever going to come along. And you're waiting for Miss Perfect, but she doesn't exist. And..." he stopped and turned to her nervously, since he had been going on and on and had no idea what her reaction to this news would be.

Samantha didn't look overly concerned, she had a puzzled expression on her face when she moved closer to him in the car and put her arms around his and gave it a squeeze. "You don't have to explain any ancient history to me—" she started, but he interrupted.

"But that's what I'm trying to tell you. It's—" he still didn't get to finish.

"It's all right. What we have here, if I may be so bold as to say we have something starting here—"

"I think so," he interjected.

"What we have here is very nice. I don't care what happened before you were introduced to me and, to be honest, there is nothing to tell you about what happened in the romance department to me before I met you. Unless of course that bothers you, that I am not experienced?" she questioned and he seemed to relax.

"Hardly! From the moment I saw you get off that elevator it felt like my best friend came back from a long trip. I don't know how to explain it. It just felt right that we were together. That we are together. I just want to be careful."

"Kenny, I have been careful all my life and I don't want to be that way anymore. I know all I need to know about your love life, unless, of course, you have some sort of disease or something?" she asked as she sat up straight, let her arms drop and looked out the windshield to see the snow capped mountains in the distance.

"No. All set there," he said with a laugh. She joined in and settled back in beside him.

"Okay. We are agreed then. Now on to your life story telling!" she encouraged.

"Boy are you going to regret this. You know lawyers get paid by the word."

"I am fully prepared to hear your voice for the entire trip. Stop stalling - Why is your real name Kenny?" she prodded.

"Well I can't start there. First I have to explain about my Mother. She is a rather-unique individual, shall I say? You know what, I meant to grab a soda before I left. Would you mind if we got off at Taft Corner and got something?"

"You are really too much," she said pretending to be annoyed. "I'm never going to hear a thing about this lady, am I? Do you even have a Mother? Are we really going to Boston to see her? You're not a serial killer, are you?" she joked as he got off the exit and pulled into the first gas station/convenience store they found.

"Very funny, Mr. Seinfeld. Do you want anything?" he asked before heading into the store.

"I'll take a Diet Coke, but who's Seinfeld?"

"Oh brother, I do have alot to teach you, don't I?" he said in mock disgust, shaking his head.

Chapter 41

Soon he was back beside her and they were hurtling down the Interstate toward Boston. After several more attempts to distract her, he finally gave in and started to recount the story of his childhood.

It didn't surprise her to hear that he came from money - very old New England money. At least his mother was wealthy. He spoke of her with a smile pasted on his face and would nod his head vigorously and slap his leg whenever he thought of another great "Mother" story. Kenny spoke of a very beautiful, carefree girl who was the only child of a doting, devoted couple. Although she hadn't realized it, her life had been a very sheltered one.

When she was sixteen, she had fallen hard for one of her father's factory foreman. There was never any question as far as she was concerned. She knew what she wanted and she would get it, as she had everything else she had ever desired. Against her family's wishes, Piper was married the day after her eighteenth birthday. It wasn't that they objected to her choice based on his position in society (or the lack thereof); in fact, it was somewhat the opposite. They knew that Ryan Tucker was no gold digger or laze about looking for a free ride. He was what they feared the most in a son-in-law. A decent, hard working man who they couldn't have been prouder of if he had been their own son; however, they knew that he would spend every waking minute proving his worth to them, instead of concentrating on making their precious daughter happy.

Six months before the wedding, Piper had been ensconced at the family hideaway on the Seacoast of Maine. It was everyone's hope that the time away from Ryan would cool her desire for him. The distance eliminated any possibility of visits, since he refused to take any more vacation time than the week that would be their honeymoon. She never wavered in her commitment to Ryan and he never doubted that he could work with her father and make his empire quadruple in value.

The wedding took place as scheduled, but then tragedy struck during the reception. A messenger arrived to tell Piper's father that there was a fire at the shoe factory. Her father, new husband and most of the male guests disappeared as the women were left to listen to the orchestra alone in terrified silence. Piper was more annoyed, than worried. Her mother started weeping the minute she saw Ryan's face when he returned after six hours with his tuxedo in shreds and his exposed skin all blackened from the smoke. Piper tried to make jokes about his attire, the fact that the food was cold and the music was long gone, but Ryan just knelt in front of her holding her hands and staring at her with such pity in his eyes. Finally, she laughed and said, "Well out with it. What is it? Do we have to cancel the honeymoon too?"

As gently as he could, he told the love of his life that the man they both worshiped, her beloved father, had been killed by a falling beam, as he tried to rescue a child. A child who had run in the burning building after her brother. The town had been devastated by the experience for many reasons. They lost two of their own, a valuable business that had employed 85% of the population and a good, kind benefactor.

Piper never cried, nor spoke of the day or her father again. She only acknowledged the pain with one concession. From that day forward, she never wore shoes. Whenever she needed to leave the house, her feet were covered with slippers only. Not an easy accomplishment for someone who lived in Massachusetts during the winter months!

Ryan had thrown himself even more wholeheartedly (if that was possible) into rebuilding his father-in-law's dream and Piper retreated into a world of loneliness where alcohol supplied the only relief. That was until the day that she gleefully found herself pregnant. For seven months she steered clear of the drink and took care of herself like she had never done in her life. She was so happy that at last she would have someone to take care of, someone who needed her. A baby would accept her love and return it unquestioningly. A baby of hers wouldn't care about money or business or anything that she didn't care about. It would be wonderful.

Something didn't feel right after she had been to the doctor for one of her checkups. She doubled over in pain and fell to the floor on a day she was alone in her mansion in the country. She had given the servants the day off, because she wanted to surprise Ryan with the completed nursery. She had redecorated everything herself and she had planned a romantic picnic dinner in the room that connected to their bedroom. Luckily, the gardener had come back to check on some new seedlings and had heard the dishes crash as she fell. He arrived in time to deliver the baby. It was touch and go for several months as the baby recovered from the premature birth, but by the time he was a year old, Kenny was as healthy as any normal child his age.

* *

Kenny took a deep breath and turned to look at Samantha. He realized that she had been silent for a very long time.

"My God, do you realize that we are at the Hooksett toll booth already! And you've only got as far as your birth! I think I'm going to cry... how can you talk about this stuff so matter of factly?"

"To tell you the truth, I've heard it so many times from my Grandmother and the gardener, that it seems like a fictional bedtime story to me at this point. Well, do you want to take a break now?"

"Nice try! YOU STILL HAVEN'T TOLD ME WHY YOUR NAME IS KENNY!" She playfully put her hands around his neck and pretended to choke him.

"Hey, I'm driving here! Do you have the money for the tolls? We're almost there... where are coins? I need the coins!" he started to drive erratically between the lanes, slowing down as she tried to reach into her pocketbook for stray quarters. Finally she found what she was looking for, threw them across his chest and out the open window into the waiting basket. "Great shot!" he complimented, as he sped up and retook his normal position in the thickening traffic.

"Ok. I've tried to be patient with you, but you're getting on my nerves. Spill the beans, Kenny!"

"Alright, alright. You've worn me down. This really is the best part of the story. I'm named after the gardener..." here he paused for effect, as she leaned closer waiting for the revelation "...the gardener who delivered me... Leonard!"

"Leonard! How do you get Kenny out of Leonard?"

"Leave it to my mother. She invited him to the hospital a few days after I was born to thank him for saving both our lives. You see she was in pretty bad shape and they had to take drastic measures to stop the bleeding. She couldn't have any more kids after that and the doctors told her that if Leonard hadn't been there when she fell, we both would have died. She wanted to honor her hero by naming the baby after him. He was stunned, but managed to say that Leonard Tucker was a fine name. My mother stared at him blankly and said, 'What the hell are you talking about?' He said, 'My name ma'am. It's Leonard.' 'Haven't I always called you Kenny?' she says and he laughs and smiles shyly and says, 'Yes ma'am. But my name is Leonard. That's why most people call me LENNY.' 'Oh that's dreadful' my mother says and then shrugs and shouts, 'Kenny, it is!'"

"You expect me to believe that? You are pathetic. Now I know you are lying!"

"Believe me, within two minutes of meeting my mother you will know that I am telling the truth. She's a horse of a different color, as they say!"

Based on his recollections over the next hour, she was starting to paint quite an odd picture in her mind of the woman that she was about to meet. If he were teasing her, she would die of embarrassment. If he was telling the truth, she just might suffer the same fate. She'd find out soon enough...

Chapter 42

Kenny had talked lovingly about all that he and his mother did together, while he was growing up. She enjoyed games, so they played many variations of cards, as well as every board game ever invented. She never went to other people's parties, unless Kenny was invited. When he was small, everyone indulged Piper; however, once he was in junior high the invitations dried up-others found their relationship a tad weird.

That didn't stop others from coming to the Tucker homes for the lavish spreads put on. There was always some sort of production involving Kenny, whether he was singing, dancing or acting. Again, guests were probably more interested in getting ammunition for the rumor mills about their odd hostess, but Piper and Kenny didn't care. Long after everyone else had gone home, they would be in Kenny's room whispering and giggling, reliving the high points of the evening.

Things changed when Kenny was in high school. Ryan got very ill and summoned him to his deathbed. He apologized for being away so much of the time while he was growing up and asked for Kenny's forgiveness. Kenny gave it and assured him that Piper had provided much more than a child could ever wish for. He didn't mean for that to hurt his father, he just wanted him to die in peace, knowing that there were no chips on his shoulder.

Ryan's last wish was for Kenny to take over the family business. Knowing that this would have been the one thing to kill his mother, and therefore the last thing that his father would really want, he told him that he couldn't, because his only desire was to become an attorney. Of course this was a lie... it was the only thing that came to mind, because the muted TV in the corner of the hospital room had a courtroom drama playing. Ryan reminded his son that he had never asked him for anything and had never interfered with his relationship with Piper. He had always felt like an outsider with the two, but it was worth it to see them both so happy, because he loved them more than they could know. He asked Kenny to promise that he would be the best possible attorney. He begged him not to sit back and expect the world to cater to him the way Piper had always done. This was the mark he wanted to leave on his son and Kenny swore that he would work hard and be a success by Ryan's standards.

Samantha was overcome by many emotions as Kenny's life story wrapped up as they headed into the Boston suburb where Piper's retirement villa was located. They had led such different lives up to the point when they met and yet they seemed to be soul mates. It was comforting for her to know that Kenny had enjoyed his childhood, as much as she had hated hers. She had many questions for him, but they would have to wait until tonight. They were admitted by security into the compound that consisted of beautiful grounds surrounding a spectacular facility that Samantha imagined was not unlike the home that Kenny grew up in.

"Well, we are here. Can you believe it? I don't think I've talked so much in one sitting in my life!"

"Thank you, Kenny, for sharing all that with me. I can't wait to meet your mother. She sounds like one hell of a lady."

"Oh you're in for a treat," Kenny snickered, as he parked & then leaned over for a lingering kiss.

Samantha wondered what Kenny's mother would think of her. Would it matter? She probably hated anyone who ever got close to him, given the nature of their relationship. Of course this explained why he had never married. Oh my God... what have I gotten myself into? Inwardly she was a mess, but on the outside, she appeared cool as a cucumber. Here goes nothing, she thought, as they ran up the front steps.

Chapter 43

Samantha and Kenny were led through a maze of hallways and sitting rooms, on their way to Mrs. Tucker's suite. All of a sudden Samantha was struck with a feeling of dread. She grabbed Kenny and pulled him to a complete stop as she whispered, "Your Mom isn't... ill... is she?"

Kenny smiled and whispered back,"Noooooo, why do you ask?"

At this point the orderly or nurse that had been escorting them realized that they were not keeping up with him, so he turned around and came back to where they were standing. "We really should get going; your Mother is waiting." The tall, thin and very handsome young man was checking his watch nervously.

"Thanks Hans. We'll be right along. You don't have to baby-sit us, you know. I'm sure this place keeps you hopping with a million more important things, so why don't you run along? I just need a minute to brief the lamb that is about to go to slaughter!" Kenny playfully knocked Samantha off balance with a hip bump she wasn't expecting.

Hans seemed to relax and then slapped Kenny on the shoulder as he headed back the way they had come. "Thanks man. I'll see you in about a half hour." He winked at Samantha as he passed and said, "She's not as bad as he thinks... but she's probably a lot worse than you think!"

A small cry erupted from Samantha's throat, as the two men shared a chuckle at her expense. "You know what? I think you should probably do this alone. I'll just be in the way. Your Mom doesn't want a stranger intruding on your visit. That would be really rude. What was I thinking?" she choked out, as Kenny held her close while continuing to laugh.

"Hey - we're just kidding - it will be fine, trust me! My mother is going to LOVE you. I can feel it! Now listen, I don't know why the question about her health came out of left field, but to answer it, no, she is not ill. She's healthier than you and I put together. She'll outlive us all!"

Kenny noticed the questioning look in Samantha's eye and continued on, nodding his head. "I know what you're thinking. Why would a perfectly healthy, wealthy woman who adored her son choose to live here, three hours away from him, in a group home? We had a few tousles about this one, but I finally realized it was her way of making me keep my promise to Dad, plus maybe getting me moving in the area of grandchildren for her."

Suddenly Samantha couldn't breathe and she felt faint. She saw the look of panic on Kenny's face. "Whoa, whoa, whoa... what kind of a charade are you pulling here?" she managed to get out before collapsing into a chair lining the narrow hallway, realizing too late that perhaps this expensive furniture was not intended for actual use.

"Oh God, no! You misunderstood. It's a long story, but I'll try to give you the short and sweet version, before she sends out a rescue squad. She kept cutting herself off from me, trying to force me to forge my own way and do the lawyer-thing. She gave me the house at Bowtie Bay in Vermont, hoping that I would decide to settle down there and raise a family away from the city. If it hadn't been for my father and the business, she would have been perfectly happy to move there when I was born. Anyway, I would only go up on long weekends and I still lived with her in the Boston Brownstone, so she announces one day that she's sold every other house, apartment, etc. and she's moving into this place. The next day I received the call from Upton Sheltra and the rest is history."

"So, I'm not here to—" Kenny interrupted before she could continue.

"You are here because we are friends heading down to the Cape for the weekend and I thought it would be nice to swing by and say hello to my dear old Mommy."

They both jumped when the deep voice from around the corner asked, "To whom are you referring as old?"

Chapter 44

"There's my girl," Kenny cooed, as he jogged over to the petite, white haired lady who had scared them both. The two embraced warmly, as Samantha surveyed the matriarch she hoped desperately to impress. She was even more regal than the picture that had been forming in her mind's eye, based on all that Kenny had relayed about her.

One of the first things she noticed with surprise were the ornate white slippers that graced her delicate feet. "I told you," Kenny whispered in her ear as he brushed past. "Mother, I'd like you to meet—"

"Oh my dear she needs no introduction," Mrs. Tucker chastised Kenny, as she held out her hands for Samantha to grasp while welcoming her with a wide smile. "I've heard a lot about you—"

"Hey, shouldn't we get back to your salon? I'm sure Hans has quite a spread ready to greet us, eh?" Kenny interrupted nervously. His manner was not lost on either of the women; both gave him puzzled looks and they exclaimed, "What is the matter with you?" at the same moment.

The coincidence seemed to break the tension and they all laughed easily. "Well, I suppose we can hold the chatter until we are safely tucked away in my prison," Piper whimpered, although she slyly winked at Samantha, "since my son seems to be embarrassed by my public appearance."

"That is not even funny, mother!" Kenny scolded, shaking his finger at her and then following that with another hug. "You know very well that you have never looked less than perfect in public and at no time in my life have you ever embarrassed me! I just haven't even had a chance to formally introduce you to my friend, SAMANTHA, and already you are going to tell tales out of school! That's hardly fair."

Samantha heard the emphasis on her name and saw the fleeting, confused look on his mother's face. There wasn't time for analysis, however, because Piper quickly put her arm in Samantha's and quite strongly pulled toward the aforementioned destination at a rapid pace. "Oh Kenny?" she teasingly threw over her shoulder, "Didn't I teach you that life isn't always fair?"

He laughed softly and followed the duo down the hall, shaking his head and running his fingers through his hair. His mother was acting as tour guide along the way, offering little known tidbits about the art work that adorned the walls, as well as the "inmates" occupying the unseen areas behind them. Samantha liked Piper immediately and found herself looking forward to spending some time with her. Looks could certainly be deceiving. A first glance at Kenny's mom would have one think that she was a frail, old (and probably confused) woman. Samantha knew from the feel of her arm in hers that physically she was very strong and she sensed that mentally it was more of the same.

By the time the group arrived at her apartment, they had been treated to more in depth facts than they would have thought possible. The rooms were very elaborate and expensively furnished. Samantha tried to drink in all the stories about Kenny and his father that had shaped Piper's decision to bring each item with her. As with her first introduction to Kenny, she immediately felt at home with this person and had no doubt that they were destined to be friends. Very good friends. And that thought brought a very broad smile to Samantha's face.

She was having a wonderful time and if she dared to admit it, she was actually close to being the happiest she had ever been in her life. The only thing that was holding her back was the look of concern on Kenny's face. It was obvious that he was keeping something from his mother and it probably involved her. Samantha couldn't decide if she wanted to know what it was or not. She finally decided that if Kenny's Mom didn't pursue it, she wouldn't either. She felt she could rely on this woman's judgment. It had been a long time since she had trusted anyone, and yet here she was with two people that she hadn't even known six months ago. She felt completely out of control, but at ease. She decided this was a good feeling. She would try it more often!

Chapter 45

It only seemed like fifteen minutes had gone by, but when Samantha looked at her watch, she couldn't believe that they had been there for almost an hour visiting. Piper had asked questions non-stop and Samantha realized that she had been on the hot seat for most of the time talking about her work and life. She hadn't minded at all, which was odd, considering that clients had grilled her for years and peppered her with constant personal questions that she always managed to elude with ease.

She enjoyed explaining about captives, as well as the history of Champlain Risk Systems. She could tell from the look on Piper's face that she didn't quite follow the logic behind the business. Samantha was very familiar with this facial expression, as it was pasted on every job applicant throughout the entire interview process. She often tried to imagine what was going on inside their heads, something like "Just do well in this meeting and you'll have time to find out what the hell she is talking about before you start work!"

Samantha was certain that Piper was less concerned with the insurance talk and more interested in the looks that were exchanged between her and Kenny, as well as how they constantly interrupted each other and playfully finished each other's sentences. Just as Samantha was checking her watch, Kenny had moved over to her chair and sat on the edge, while putting his arm around her shoulders.

"I hate to break this up, girls," he drawled, "but I am one hungry cowboy! Are we going to eat today, Mother?"

"Oh my heavens! Some hostess I am. I'm sorry kids, I completely forgot." She turned to Samantha and offered, "You must be overdue for a visit to the little girl's room... please help yourself to anything in there you need to freshen up and then seat yourself in the dining room and start without us. Luckily I had Armand bring in only cold salads, so everything should still be ok."

Kenny helped her to her feet and then kissed her on the cheek to his mother's amusement, "That sounds like a plan. We'll be right along, I just want to talk business with my mother for a few minutes before we join you."

"Oh darling, I'm so glad you don't mind. I do have a few personal estate problems I need to run by my favorite attorney and I don't want to bore Samantha to tears."

They both were walking Samantha out of the room so fast she had no doubts that they would soon be talking about her. Oh well, she thought. They are bound to do it sooner or later, so let it be now. I have a feeling I passed inspection with flying colors!

She reached the bathroom and was overwhelmed by the size of it. It certainly was easy to forget that she was in a retirement home-everything was so elegant she was starting to feel insecure again. Since she could only hear the pitches of the voices in the other room and not any words, she decided to close the door and concentrate on examining all that was before her. She had no idea what half of the items were on the bathroom shelf, to say nothing of whether she needed or wanted to use them. She set about opening all the bottles and sniffing the contents. In seconds she was oblivious to what might be happening in the next room.

Chapter 46

Piper counted to ten after Samantha closed the door and then practically leapt across the room toward her son. Through clenched teeth she whispered loudly, "What the Hell is going on? Where is Cinnamon?" as she repeatedly slapped him in the head, arm & stomach.

"God dammit, Mother, will you give me a second to explain?" he managed to get out between dodging her blows.

"Yes Kenny Tucker, I will give you a second to explain. You take a second to explain to me how I have heard nothing but glowing reports for A YEAR about your girlfriend. Please explain why you called me a month ago and made me the happiest woman in the world when you said you were FINALLY going to ask her to marry you and that you would FINALLY bring her down to meet me. Now let me think, when was that supposed to happen? Oh that's right-today! Then please, dear boy, explain to me why you show up with someone named Samantha that you can't keep your hands off!!!! What am I missing here? Are engagements handled differently these days? After all, I will have to count on you to enlighten me, since I'm more familiar with the courting rituals from the last century. Please, enlighten me!"

Kenny had moved to the love seat and sat with his head in his hands the entire time that Piper was circling the room exasperated. When he didn't respond, she took a moment to control her breathing and then padded quietly over and sat down next to him. She placed her hands on the sides of his face and gently lifted until his eyes met hers.

She was reminded of how much she loved this son of hers and she felt terrible for not allowing him a chance to speak. "I'm sorry. Forgive me," was all she could think of to say. He looked so tormented that she couldn't imagine what was going on in his head.

Kenny pulled his mother close and kissed the top of her head for a long time. He stood up, turned to face her and indicated with his hands that she should stay seated.

"A lot has happened since I talked to you-obviously." He was speaking softly and gesturing to the dining room where Samantha was presumably eating. "I want to tell you all about it. I NEED your opinion and advice about everything. But this isn't going to be easy. Not for either of us. I brought Sam because I thought it would explain-that somehow you'd understand better. Or maybe I wanted you to tell me that I did the right thing or that I made the biggest mistake of my life. God, I don't know anymore!"

"It's alright, dear. It is. See? I'm calm now. You're ok. Let's just sit down and talk about what's bothering you. Come on. Spill it!" Piper struggled to smile, as her voice was shaking and her heart was beating in her ears.

"One condition, Mom. I want to start at the beginning and tell you everything. All at once-no interruptions. Can you just listen now and save your comments/questions for the end? Can you possibly do that?" By his expression it was clear that he doubted it.

His mother straightened her back and squared her shoulders before responding, "I tell everyone here what a good listener I am. I don't anticipate a problem with your request."

Kenny laughed nervously and rolled his eyes, but then he launched excitedly into what he had been practicing over and over in his mind the entire drive down. Not an easy task, considering that he was actually talking to Samantha at the same time!

He started pacing back and forth across the room, something he was sure would drive his mother insane, but he was too nervous to sit in a chair, and he didn't want to look in her eyes as he spoke.

"I don't have to tell you, Mom, that from a very early age I was positive that my future involved a family-well, children at least."

"I know that—"

"Mom, please! I said start to finish-not a word!"

Piper caught herself before a "Sorry!" slipped out and simply made a motion like a key locking her mouth. She slumped against the back of her seat, with her eyes closed for a moment. She held out her hand to indicate that Kenny should proceed.

He began, "You know how much I loved growing up with you and I always knew that someday I would share the same type of upbringing with offspring. In college I wasn't anxious to settle down, but who is? I had a wonderful time and met a lot of fascinating women, but not once did I think, 'Is she THE one?' When I was in law school, more of the same. Great women-good friends, but never anything serious. When I had been working for a few years, I thought it was time to look for a candidate to be the mother of my children. The only problem was that by that time, every woman I met had no desire for marriage or kids. Time went by quickly. I was aging, but I never doubted that I would still have everything that I had always dreamed of. If anything, I felt even stronger that things would eventually be as I wanted.

"The pictures in my head became more and more detailed. I would fall asleep at night, dreaming of the birth of my son, Ryan Piper—" at this point Kenny stopped and turned to check on his mother. He had heard the sigh, when the name that he had picked out for his first born had been uttered. Piper's eyes were moist and she took a handkerchief from an unseen hiding spot in her sleeve (he had never known his mother to be far removed from a tissue in a crisis), but she did not interrupt him. Whether it was the mention of his father, who she still missed deeply, or the fact that her grandson would be forever linked to her via a shared name, he didn't know, but he continued.

"I would do it all from the birth experience, to the diapers and midnight feedings. I'd sleep in his room at night, to provide protection from monsters and he'd have all that he could possibly need or want. I'd quit my job and stay home. I'd teach him everything from the ABCs and 123s to hunting and fishing. We'd play hard all day long and sleep deep all night through. There would never be a single regret.

"Exactly three years later, he would be joined by his sister, Lindsey Ellen. We'd call her Ellie, you know, L.E.?" Piper nodded her understanding.

"Little Ryan would love helping me with the baby and I'd do it all over again, but this time it would be different, because it would be my little girl, my angel. Instead of my rough and tumble little man." Kenny stopped in front of a table that held a pitcher of water and poured a glass for himself.

He didn't offer any to Piper, but she was too keyed up to drink anything anyway. As he took a long drink, she wondered if he had a lump in his throat, the size of the one she had. They had never talked about this and she was touched that he had wanted to have children as much (if not more) than she had wanted grandchildren. She had no idea. It was very difficult for her to hold her tongue, but she vowed not to utter a word, until he requested it.

"Time passed and the images would only get stronger. I could see exactly what they looked like and I could feel their arms around my neck and their kisses on my cheek. What I couldn't see-not with one woman that I ever spent any time with, was their mother. In my mind, it was always only the three of us. In reality, I never found a partner that shared my vision. If they wanted children, it was never their idea for me to quit work; in fact, most of them weren't planning to quit work either. What would be the point? Having children to be taken care of by Nannies until they were old enough to be sent away to Boarding School? I didn't want that. I don't want that.

"But I never doubted that I would find somebody. Never. You know what though? Time has a way of playing tricks on you. One day you wake up and you're fifty-five years old. You're thinking about quitting work, not because you're going to stay home and raise your children, but because you're almost at retirement age and what's the point? You have no children. What are you working for? You have enough money, Hell, you've always had more than enough money. You have respect, accomplishments, friends..." Kenny's voice trailed off and then he shook his head and cleared his throat. He had a long way to go and was unsure how long his mother could sit by without comment, so he plunged on.

"I had been dating Ginger for awhile. That's her name, Mother, Ginger-not Cinnamon. She is a sweet girl and I do care about her-I may even love her, I don't know. She wasn't thrilled about the idea of children when I first brought it up, but she didn't reject it outright. When I told her I was thinking of quitting my new job and moving to Bowtie Bay permanently, she didn't react about the money aspect. In fact, she told me to do whatever would make me happy. I know she loves me. I guess that's what made this so difficult. It wasn't right, I do know that, but I decided to ask her to marry me. Do you know why?"

Piper shook her head, but didn't say a word or take her gaze off Kenny for an instant.

"Because one night I went to bed and dreamt that Ryan and Lindsey were missing. I couldn't find them anywhere. I woke up in a panic, because the nightmare was that they didn't exist. I had waited too long, so they would never exist." Kenny finished the water from the glass that he still held tightly in his hand; Piper worried that he was holding it so that it would burst and he would be cut, but she sat unmoving and silent.

"That day I went to the jewelry store and (unfortunately) bought a ring from Ginger's friend, Mark. I was planning to ask her that night. Remember? I called you that morning after I left the store." He didn't wait for an acknowledgment. Even though he was turned away from his mother, she could sense that the toughest part of the story was yet to come.

"I had a luncheon scheduled with one of my partners. I almost blew it off, because I wanted to go home and make everything perfect for my proposal, but I didn't. And that changed everything." Kenny looked at the dining room door and some of the color returned to his face. He smiled and Piper felt some of the tension in the room released, although she was bracing herself for more bad news.

"Carlene, my partner, had to cancel. As luck, or fate or whatever would have it, another one of our lawyers had canceled a lunch with Samantha. We both were there, so we decided to stay and have lunch anyway. Mom, I can't even tell you how I felt from the INSTANT I saw her get off the elevator. It was like she was a piece of me that I had lost a long time ago. We could talk and joke easily. I can't describe how I felt spending the day with her." Kenny checked his mother and as he suspected saw a rather disgusted look on her face.

"Believe me, I know what you're thinking. It was just panic. I didn't really want to make a commitment, so I would have jumped at any opportunity for an excuse. If Ma Kettle had shown up at that moment, I would have been head over heels for her."

Piper smiled while thinking that Ma Kettle had always reminded her of her Mother-in-law, whom she had loved dearly. She started to share this with Kenny, but then rethought it. She relaxed and waited for him to continue.

"Yes. We spent the day together. One thing led to another—" seeing the look of horror on his mother's face, he screamed, "God no! Not that. No we didn't sleep together, in fact we still haven't." He could tell that Piper was momentarily relieved by this revelation, even if the frank discussion was leaving her a bit squeamish.

"No. We talked for hours. We club hopped-played pool, went dancing. She had never had alcohol before and I inadvertently got her drunk (another story that isn't relevant right now)! Anyway, she fell asleep or passed out, I guess, and had this nightmare that had her screaming hysterically. This is terrible, I realize that now. But I know that if that had happened with Ginger, I would have said, 'Ok crazy lady, see ya around'. But all I wanted to do was find out what was wrong and fix it somehow. It's not like me! I have never invested so much into a relationship (except for you, of course) and I had just met her!

"Anyway... She basically told me to get lost, but I wouldn't. I took her home and made her tell me everything. I can't believe what she has gone through. You have to know how incredible it is that she is as stable as she is. Her childhood was nonexistent. Her parents were high schoolers who were forced to get married after her Mom got pregnant. Her dad deserted the family when she was three and her mother hung herself when she was five—"

"Kenny please stop!" Piper cried, as she buried her face in her hands. "I can't listen to any more of this."

Kenny knelt down in front of her and stroked her hair. "I'm sorry, but yes you can. I know you can. You're strong like she is. That's why I want you to hear this. I want you to understand and I was hoping maybe you could help me understand. I shouldn't have—"

"Wait. I'm the one who is sorry. You're right, of course. If this poor girl has lived it, I can certainly listen to it. Go on." Piper squeezed his hand and released it, so he could continue his job of destroying her carpet.

The pacing resumed as he said, "I'm almost done, believe it or not. She was shut off physically from her father's parents and emotionally distanced from her mother's parents, who raised her. She went to college and then only returned to Vermont to start her company, but hadn't been back home until right before we met. Her father just died (another long story) but the part that concerns us is that her paternal grandmother gave her something at the funeral. Well, actually she threw it in her face and laughed about it being her mom's suicide note."

The small cry that erupted from Piper was not lost on Kenny, but he had to finish before Samantha came to check on them. "For the last week, we've been fighting about the damn note. I've told her to either read it and be done with it or throw it away and never think of it again." He finally paused and turned to Piper waiting for some acknowledgment that she was following, but was greeted with another confused look instead.

Sensing that it was now ok for her to comment, Piper struggled to her feet and indicated that Kenny should sit on the love seat. He shook his head, but she took his arm and said, "You've had your say. Now it's my turn. I insist you be seated, before I lose my mind with your incessant speed racing around this room. I'm going to ask some questions and you will be allowed to answer. Then I'm going to speak my mind and you are going to listen without an interruption. Do you understand?”

He didn’t argue.

Chapter 47

"Please indulge me, as I fill in a few blanks," she stated, while taking a few steps to relieve the stiffness in her joints. "Does Nutmeg know about Samantha?"

Kenny shook his head uncomfortably and shifted in his seat before saying quietly, "When I got home that morning, after spending the night with Samantha (TALKING, mother!) Ginger was waiting for me. She was hysterical. She thought I had been lying in the proverbial ditch all night. Once she saw that I was all right, she just was so happy, she didn't even pursue the 'where the hell were you and what the fu—funny business, heck were you doing?' routine.

"I was half hoping that she would be furious and scream all sorts of outrageous accusations at me; you know, something that I could respond to with indignation. Then she would tell me that everything was over between us, because she couldn't trust me. I would act terribly hurt and then she would leave and it would be done. But of course I was just being a selfish coward."

"Well at least you realize that," Piper harrumphed. "Go on," she said with annoyance in her voice.

Kenny couldn't shake the look of Ginger's face out of his mind. She was so young and beautiful. Her long black hair cascaded onto her shoulders, where her year 'round tan gleamed from underneath her sleeveless dress. Her bright blue eyes so filled with life and that perfect mouth. Those full lips curving into that gorgeous smile. Her white teeth dazzling, her flawless complexion gleaming.

He had no complaints with her body either. She had been a track star in college and had kept herself in training shape for the last two years. He loved the way her magnificent breasts heaved when she ran. Often on the weekends he would bring a book or a legal brief to the university, to watch from the stands as she circled the infield.

Of course he never actually read anything he brought, he simply pretended. Not once had he failed to get a hard on just observing her from afar. They would always go back to his place after and make love. But of late, he found it difficult to hold off coming. The last time (God it seemed so long ago now) he had barely gotten his pants off, because the sight of her removing the sweat soaked bra and freeing her enlarged nipples had been too much for him.

Kenny realized with embarrassment that a bulge was forming in his trousers, as he was standing before his mother. His face flamed with disgust; he turned toward the buffet in the corner and used his arms to prop himself up and away.

Most of his friends had wives like Ginger, but they were second or third versions. Kenny knew what they felt for them was the same that he felt for her. It wasn't love. It was pure lust. The combination of sexual desire and the satisfaction of attaining someone younger and more beautiful than one's partners could not be overrated. It was more important than legal ability. It was more important than the power to change lives. It was too important and Kenny hadn't realized it until that moment.

He had never been as comfortable with Ginger, as he had been that first night with Samantha. It wasn't about sex; it was about being able to carry on a conversation with someone who understands what you are saying. It was about having the same belief system and caring about the same things in life. He knew then that he had never believed Ginger belonged with him. But he did feel that way about Samantha. She fit into what he wanted his life to be-not what it had become.

"Are you alright?" Piper asked from across the room, jarring Kenny out of his daydreaming.

"Yeah, I'm sorry. I was just thinking about Ginger. She didn't get mad, you know, which made me all the madder. I told her that we couldn't see each other any more and she started to laugh. When I didn't say anything, she let me know that Mark had called her after I bought the ring and spilled the beans. I didn't have to play games because she knew that we were getting married.

She started dancing around the room, singing, 'Yes, Yes of course I'll marry you.'

She had already called her parents, grandparents-God, even her best friend Carol, who she wanted to be her maid of honor. I kept saying, Ginger, I made a mistake, it's over, but she wouldn't listen to me!

"Finally I grabbed her and screamed, I can't marry you! Don't you understand? There's someone else! She wouldn't believe me. Again, she was so calm and insistent, not angry at all. When it finally started to sink in, she tried to seduce me. I'm sure I don't have to go into that..." he asked, with a hopeful glance back at Piper.

"Please don't, thank you," she said while rolling her eyes and trying to look as matronly as possible.

"Anyway, the important thing is that she basically was standing there with all her clothes off when Samantha's ex-(I don't know what you would call her), personal assistant, I guess-showed up."

"Oh good Lord," said Piper, as she went to the beverage cart and poured herself a scotch. "What's next in this soap opera?"

Kenny rethought the idea of asking Piper not to drink and instead poured himself one as well. "Jeannie left before we could say anything, but of course you know she had a completely wrong idea in her head. It finally dawned on Ginger that I was serious. After a few exclamations about what a struggle it would be to try and pick up her shattered life at the veteran age of twenty-four she took off. I haven't seen her since."

"And what does Samantha know about all this?" Piper inquired, knowing full well the answer.

Kenny drained his drink and sat down hard, "I told her on the way down that I wanted to be honest with her and I started to explain, but she wouldn't let me. She said that whatever happened before we met didn't matter and she wasn't interested. I tried to get out that it wasn't exactly ancient history, but she was really quite insistent."

Piper chastised Kenny with her eyes before saying, "Oh you poor, powerless, little chicken shit... whatever will you do?"

"MOTHER!" Kenny snapped as his face turned white and his jaw dropped.

"Oh please, dear boy. Wake up! It's not like you two are moving to a deserted island and will never chance upon these people again. She has to be told and you know it!" Piper saw the questioning look in his eyes and for the first time in her life was truly annoyed with her son. "You can't think that I'll tell her for you?"

"The thought had entered my mind," said Kenny with a smirk. "Don't you think that would be best?"

"No I don't and I am insulted and disappointed that you would even suggest a thing!"

"I'm sorry, forget it. I know what I have to do, but I just wanted to check that I wasn't misreading the woman's perspective on this one, as far as full disclosure!" Neither could resist the other's charms, so they shared a hug and then were both reseated on the couch.

Piper took a deep breath and then asked, "One more question and then I think we need to check on Samantha." Kenny saw what time it was and winced. "You said something about her mother's suicide note causing problems for you two... What's that all about?"

In an instant, Kenny was back on his feet pacing. "Here's where I'm confused. Her Mom hung herself three DECADES ago and Sam has been able to put all the pain and hurt behind her and become a very successful entrepreneur. She's attractive, wealthy and sane, in spite of everything. What possible difference to her life could that note make now? She's not going to change who she is or lose anything based on something that has been hidden for all these years. Why can't she just read it or throw it away? I don't understand."

Both Kenny and Piper jumped unexpectedly at the sound of the dining room door opening. It was hard to tell who was more uncomfortable, the guilty duo, interrupted while talking about their guest; or Samantha, positive that she was intruding on a private conversation that was too intense and personal for a stranger to hear.

"I'm really sorry to bother you, but I was starting to get worried when I realized that I ate most of the food that was probably intended for all three of us." Samantha attempted a smile, but the forced laughter of Kenny and Piper made her withdraw it.

It was Piper who recovered first and asked Kenny, "Won't you be a dear and go get me some onion rings from Allouetta's?"

"What? Onion Rings? From where?" Kenny asked confused.

"You know that place in Revere, silly!" She turned to Samantha and offered, "It's known far and wide for those tasty treats."

Kenny smiled at Sam and asked Piper mockingly, "Do you mean Angeleno's Clams?"

"Yes, yes, yes. Of course, that's it," said Piper as she directed Kenny to the door. "You know how I get something in my head and then I just have to have it! Don't be long, now."

"Do you want to come with me, Sam?" Kenny asked, after managing to stick his foot in the door to stop Piper from slamming it in his face. He struggled to indicate with his eyebrows that it was very important for her survival to accompany him.

"Oh don't be ridiculous," exclaimed Piper, looking over her shoulder at Samantha and making a face, "You know the way all by your lonesome and us girls need a chance to get to know each other. Bye, bye now."

"Mother, I don't think—" Kenny started, but it was too late. Piper had already closed the door while answering, "Well that's the problem, dear. We know you don't think."

Samantha had to laugh; half from sheer panic at being alone with this icon and half because she truly enjoyed her spirit.

"OK, my sweet," began Piper within seconds of Kenny's abrupt departure, "we don't have much time. Fill me in on your intentions towards my son!"

Samantha wasn't laughing anymore...

Chapter 48

Samantha eyed the two scotch glasses and was interested in dirtying a third, but decided against it. She was sure she needed to keep a clear head to get through this inquisition.

"My intentions?" Samantha giggled nervously. "To be honest I haven't known your son long enough to have any intentions." She looked at Piper hopefully, "Does that answer your question?"

Piper laughed also, putting Samantha at ease. "I'm just teasing, dear. I know my son. I'm sure he filled you with horror stories about me the whole trip down here, so I didn't want you to go home disappointed."

"Well thank you. I'll be sure to tell him how terrifying this experience has been." She accepted Piper's outstretched hand and they walked together into the dining room.

"Oh my," exclaimed Piper, when she saw the empty dishes, "you weren't joking when you said you were hungry!"

Samantha's face turned purple with embarrassment, as she recalled all the delicious food. "I am so sorry," she said, "but you guys were talking for a very long time!"

Piper nodded and became serious again. "Yes, we were and I hope you aren't upset, but he told me a lot about you... personally." She took a long time drawing out the last word, as she peered at Samantha from underneath her lowered eyelashes.

"I see," responded Samantha. "What is it they say, just because you're paranoid, doesn't mean they aren't talking about you or some such thing?" She walked to the picture window and drank in the view of the well-manicured grounds. With her back to Kenny's mother, she continued, "I suppose you have a lot of questions for me? It's ok. Ask me anything you want. I assure you, if I don't want to answer, I won't."

Piper smiled. She liked this woman a lot. It was obvious why Kenny would be drawn to her. As much as it hurt to let her dreams of grandchildren go, she understood why he made the choice he did. Now she felt it was her responsibility to make sure he didn't screw this relationship up.

"Tell me about your Mother's suicide note," she said quickly, before she changed her mind.

Samantha felt as if she had been punched in the stomach. "Boy, you don't beat around the bush, do you?" she said.

"I don't believe in wasting time. Life is too short," she stated simply, as she joined her at the window.

"Well then, let's get started," Samantha responded, without turning toward Piper. "I'll just assume that Kenny told you everything he knows, so that leaves very little. My mother hung herself when I was five. My grandparents had taken me school shopping. When we got back, my dad's parents were there. They had found her. It never bothered me that she didn't leave a note. I guess because I felt that somehow we were so close, she knew that she didn't have to explain. I don't know. It sounds ridiculous now that I've said it out loud. Anyway, it turns out she did leave a note. For some reason, my grandmother withheld it for all these years to protect me. But now, since she hates me, she suddenly doesn't care to have my feelings spared.

"I've been carrying the stupid thing around with me for weeks now. Kenny can't understand why I don't just read it or throw it away and I haven't been able to explain to him why it's more complicated than that." She was suddenly very tired and sat down at the table and poured a glass of water for herself, although she didn't drink it, she just played with the tumbler.

"Men are idiots most of the time," Piper declared, "but what can you do?"

"Do YOU understand? Or are you Kenny's delegate to get me moving one way or the other?" Her eyes searched Piper's face. She desperately wanted this woman to understand-even more than she wanted Kenny to. In fact, if Piper could assure her that waiting to decide what to do without rushing into anything was sound, then it wouldn't matter at all what Kenny thought.

Piper sat down opposite her and waited to respond. "I do understand." She patted Samantha's hand and smiled warmly. "And you know what? I know exactly how to get Kenny to understand too. Leave it all to me."

Chapter 49

It was getting dark by the time Piper and Samantha heard Kenny's return. They hadn't noticed that an hour and a half had flown by, because they had been engrossed talking.

The two women quickly picked up on Kenny's disgusted look, as well as the fact that he didn't have anything in his hands. His mission had failed for one reason or another.

"Mother," Kenny began with false sweetness, "did you know all along that Angeleno's closed months ago?"

"Oh that's right, sorry darling. No matter, onion rings are bad for you anyway. You really should give them up my dear." She stared at Kenny and then looked to Samantha for confirmation.

Kenny shook his head in disbelief and started to head to the dining room. "Well I hope you guys got to know each other. If you'll excuse me, I'm going to grab something to eat. I'm STILL starving." He stopped to glare at his mother.

Piper gave him a hug and then turned him around quickly and led him back to the door. "Sorry, but Armand came and picked up the plates already. You missed out while you were out fooling around. That will teach you," she added, while turning to wink at Samantha.

"Mother, sometimes you are so trying," Kenny said exhausted.

"I know, sweetie, that's why you put me in this home—" she teased, but Kenny interrupted very agitated.

"That is a lie and you know it! Samantha what has she been telling you? I think I better get you out of here, so I can debrief you." The minute it escaped his mouth, he wished he could take the words back.

Piper immediately countered with, "well I don't know about the briefs, Kenny, but I can tell that the underwire bra she's wearing has become a real pain."

Both Kenny and Samantha were shocked, but then collapsed into uncontrollable laughter, along with Piper.

Samantha embraced Kenny's mother and gave her a kiss on the cheek. She thanked her, to which Piper's whispered reply was, "I'm not done yet.

"Oh Kenny, I've been meaning to tell you that your real father has been bugging me about getting you to visit him." She waited in anticipation of Kenny's response.

Samantha had no intention of waiting to see him have a stroke. She quickly said, "I'll leave you two alone," and pointed outside as Kenny struggled to breath.

* *

No more than five minutes had passed, when the door opened and Kenny emerged. His face was flushed, as he gave Samantha a deep hug. "Take as much time as you need to decide whether or not to read your Mom's note. I'm sorry I pressured you. Believe me, NOW I understand."

He was off down the hall shaking his head, before she could ask him what was going on.

But what was that all about??????

Chapter 50

The silence was deafening in the car, as Kenny sped out the entrance and headed for the Cape. Samantha wasn't sure if she should break the silence or wait for him to.

Since she had no intention of spending the rest of the weekend wondering where their relationship stood, she took a chance on a comedic tension breaker.

"You know this underwire really is killing me," she stated evenly as she looked out her window. She felt his eyes on her, so she slowly turned with a wide grin on her face. His stern expression melted and they both chuckled softly.

"She IS something else, but you know, we had a wonderful chat while you were-uh, away," she murmured, hoping the reference to his wild goose chase would not put him back into a glum mood.

"I'll bet!" he exclaimed, as he wove in and out of the traffic. "I suppose you want to hear all about her latest bomb?" Kenny asked, while staring ahead intently.

"Only if you want to tell me. I'm the last person on earth to push someone to talk about their personal issues," Samantha expressed as she turned in her seat to face him.

He seemed to relax and also slowed the car to within a few miles of the speed limit. "First things first," he said determinedly, "what did you and my lovely mother discuss while I was-uh, away?"

"Well let me see if I can recall," she joked, while tapping her finger against her cheek. "I think she waited until you closed the door before she asked me what I thought about my mother killing herself and my father deserting me."

"I'm sorry," Kenny said. He reached for her hand, squeezed it gently and then brought it to his lips for a light kiss. Instead of releasing it, he continued to hold on, resting it on his right thigh.

"Don't be," Samantha assured him, "I didn't mind at all. She was very kind and I felt very comfortable with her. Like I have known her for a very long time. The same way I feel about you. I don't pretend to understand it, but I must admit I like it. I like it very much. I hope you don't mind?" she questioned.

"Not at all," he answered. "Did she say anything about me?"

Samantha detected a change in his demeanor again. He was back on the defensive. "No she didn't," she said softly, "well nothing substantial, that is. Just the usual, my son is the greatest human being that has ever walked the earth. You know, that sort of crap!"

"Oh you're a funny lady," Kenny laughed. "Maybe I'll tell you about the crap she shared with me later on. Right now, however, I'd like to concentrate on how (and when) I'm going to get you out of that uncomfortable medieval contraption." His glance lingered on her chest; Samantha could feel her face becoming flushed.

"How much longer before we reach the Bed and Breakfast," she asked with a shaky voice, hoping that it was only her imagination and she didn't actually say the word 'bed' extremely loud.

"Patience, my friend. You'll be able to get your hot little hands on me in no time. But, please, can we eat first? I swear I'm about ready to faint!" He looked so pathetic that Samantha had to laugh.

She thought he would lose control of the car when she steadily unbuttoned her blouse to her waist and exposed the offending garment. "You can go to the dining room if you want; I'll just wait in the room. You don't mind if I start without you?" she said wickedly, as she ran her fingers underneath the compressed flesh of her bosom.

"Who could eat at a time like this?" Kenny said in mock seriousness. "I better get you undressed ASAP. This could be a very serious condition. You may have to go without clothing for twenty-four hours. Whatever will we do?"

She was surprised to see that they had arrived at the Black Raven Inn already and Kenny was skillfully parking the car in the back lot, out of sight of passersby. Within seconds of the key turning the motor off, his seatbelt had been removed and he was touching her everywhere his body could reach. Samantha ached to be with him, but not now and not like this. She kissed his neck and ear, playfully tickling his chest through the open shirt. Her hands ran through his hair when he bent to bury his face in between her breasts, but before he could go any further, she managed to push him back to the driver's side of the car. She buttoned her blouse as he stared in disbelief.

"What am I supposed to do now?" he asked incredulously, as he motioned to the bulge in his pants.

She was out of the car in a flash and only leaned back to tease, "I guess you better carry your suitcase in front of you, when you check us in!"

Kenny was thankful that the evening sky was quite dark and the subdued lighting in the lobby didn't draw attention to anything amiss. For once a check in went smoothly and within minutes they were alone in their cupola love nest. He pushed her back onto the bed.

"You're going to pay for this," he sputtered, as he lowered himself down on her.

"Looking forward to it," she whispered, as they continued where their escapades in the car had left off. She struggled with his clothing, as he did with hers, until she had only her bra and new panties left-he, nothing at all.

"You are so beautiful," Kenny choked, as he ripped the covers back and lifted her with ease to the top of the bed.

Samantha felt tears rising to her eyes, so she closed them tightly, hoping to regain control. "No one has ever said that to me before," she said softly, nuzzling his neck and reaching down with both hands to touch him.

"I'll try to remember to tell you that everyday," he said, as he turned her slightly, so that he could unhook her bra and release its painful prisoners.

When he took first one nipple and then the other into his mouth, all thoughts of maintaining control left Samantha. She could feel his hands moving down to remove her underwear, but she couldn't tell where her hands were or why they didn't seem to work anymore. But it didn't matter. His lips were burning a path down her stomach and his hands were spreading her legs apart.

"You don't have to—" she managed to get out weakly before his tongue found her clit, causing her eyes to roll back into her head. Her back arched involuntarily and she felt as if her whole body was on fire. She kept hearing a voice saying, "Oh God, Oh my God", but it was awhile before she realized it was her own.

She could feel his strong arms holding her on to the bed; if it weren't for that, her convulsions would have landed them both on the floor. She came quickly and intensely. After the orgasm had subsided, she was suddenly very self conscious about not only being completely naked before him, but the fact that he was still erect and obviously needed a similar release. She was embarrassed that she didn't know what she should do, but Kenny continued to handle the situation.

"If you don't mind, I'd like to—" he hesitated slightly, and then smiled and continued with, "come inside for a visit. I won't be long, I promise."

She had to laugh before she said awkwardly, "Please. Let me know how I can help. I think I owe you one."

He was already inside her, slipping in easily because she was so wet. At first she just lay there watching his face, as he moved rhythmically back and forth above her, balancing the majority of his weight on his muscular arms. Then she started to move against him, harder and harder until he cried out and shook violently with his mouth agape.

"Are you alright?" she gasped, thinking that he was having a heart attack.

He smiled slightly and when he had pulled out from her and fallen hard on the bed beside her, he laughed out loud. "Oh yes, I'm quite alright, thank you. Next time take it easy on me. I'm an old man, remember?"

"Don't remind me. I thought I had killed you there for a minute."

"Thanks a lot! I was only joking," Kenny said, appearing hurt.

"I'll be more careful with you next time, I promise. How about now? Are you ready?"

Kenny stopped laughing and looked at Samantha in horror, "You've got to be kidding! I'll be lucky if I can walk before next weekend."

"Ok old man, I get the picture. I'll go downstairs and troll for young studs," she teased while curling up with her head on his chest.

"Over my dead body!" Kenny exclaimed, as he grabbed her and playfully rolled her over on her stomach.

"Promises, promises..." she giggled, as Kenny proceeded to tickle her before they started in again.

It was going to be a very long wait for Kenny's next meal.

Chapter 51

Samantha couldn't breath - someone was choking her. No. Some thing was choking her. She could feel the noose tightening around her neck and was unable to scream for help. Open your eyes, she yelled at herself. It's only a dream. You're fine. You'll see. Open your eyes!

It was very dark. She couldn't tell where she was. Wait. The trip down to the Cape with Kenny. They had made love and must have fallen asleep. She remembered now. Her eyes were getting used to the darkness and she was relieved to see him lying beside her. The sound of his soft snoring reached her ears. Everything was fine. She wasn't choking at all; however, Kenny's arm was draped over her, crushing her windpipe.

She tried to clear her throat as a way of waking him up gently, but not a sound came out. Instead, she placed her fingers underneath his arm and peeled it away from her. Their dried sweat was acting like a gluing agent, and her skin hurt from the separation.

Kenny jumped with a start and wiped a small trail of drool from the corner of his mouth as he asked, "What? What is it? You ok?"

Samantha finally found her voice and managed to croak out, "I think you were trying to crush me." She smiled at the appearance of his tousled hair and gave his back a quick kiss as she made her way to the bathroom. Her vagina was sore from the workout and her legs felt like they had hundred pound weights around her ankles, but she was extremely happy.

When she caught sight of herself in the mirror, after turning on the blazing light and experiencing a bout of temporary blindness, she hardly recognized the woman in the reflection. Kenny's words came back to her, that she was beautiful, and while at the time she had assumed it was something that a man would say in the heat of passion, for the first time ever, she honestly believed it too. She prayed silently that he wouldn't recall what she had responded, that no one had ever said that to her before. It was the truth, but she didn't want to talk about it with him.

No one had ever commented on her appearance, when she was growing up, so she just lived under the assumption that she was neither gorgeous, nor ugly, she just was. She recalled the incident that had changed her assessment.

One summer between the fourth and fifth grade, her grandparents had wanted to take a trip to Maine to see some distant relatives. Samantha had no desire to go and told them she wouldn't accompany them. Her grandmother had made an idle threat to send her to 4-H camp if she didn't agree, but Samantha called her bluff. Not one to back down from a statement, off to camp she was sent.

At first she had illusions that she could pretend to be someone else for the week-a girl who was confident in her own abilities and who could make friends easily. But the dream was quickly shattered when Samantha realized that almost everyone there belonged to the 4-H Club (she didn't) and all the other campers seemed to come with small groups of friends from their home towns (she didn't know another soul). She couldn't swim, hated working on crafts and loathed sleeping under the stars, being eaten alive by all sorts of disgusting creatures.

By the end of the week she had only had an extended conversation with one counselor and that concerned a notice he had received from the IRS. Samantha had overheard him telling the nurse that he was simply going to ignore the correspondence, so she had felt compelled to instruct him on the simple course of action needed to resolve his problem. She doubted that he would heed her advice (after all, how many ten year olds knew about waiving tax penalties?); however, she felt pleased that she had at least attempted a good deed.

On the last night, a Saturday, they had a bonfire in the middle of a field and someone brought a radio, so they could listen to music and dance. Samantha was so looking forward to leaving the hellhole the next day; she was actually enjoying herself when she noticed a very attractive older boy standing about twenty-five yards away. At the same time, two female counselors behind her started to discuss him.

Craig had been coming to the camp for years and this summer was a junior assistant. One of the women commented on how good-looking he was and the other agreed, sharing that it was not always so. He had lost over a hundred pounds in the last thirty-six months. The other counselor questioned why he appeared to only dance with ugly and/or fat girls and was assured that this was his way of bringing a little bit of sunshine into the lives of those who were suffering the way he had suffered. You'll never see him with anyone attractive, she said. Isn't that the sweetest thing you ever heard?

Samantha thought it was pretty neat, until she turned and saw him standing in front of her with a smile on his face. "Would you like to dance?" he asked, bent down to her height, with his hands on his knees. She had felt sick to her stomach and was unable to speak-she merely shook her head from side to side and slowly backed away from him. She could still feel the tightness in her face, because she had refused to remove the broad smile that was pasted on for the rest of the evening. Every so often she would think of Craig and those counselors, wondering why the memory still made her eyes sting with hot tears.

"Everything ok in there?" Kenny hollered from the other room, breaking up her recollection.

"Beautiful," she announced noting irony, while wiping away the last tears she would ever shed for that little girl's pain. She emerged from the bathroom shyly, wanting to cover up her nakedness. But there was no way to hide the smile from her lips. This one was for real. And it would be for keeps.

Chapter 52

Kenny still lay on his stomach, using several pillows under his chest to prop himself up along with his arms. The blankets were in a tangled mess on the floor; the satin sheet was haphazardly thrown over his left buttock, and then wound around his thigh, calf and foot. It looked like an elegant leg cast. His hair was even more disheveled then when he first awoke, but Samantha thought he had never looked sexier.

"As exhausted as I am, pretty lady," Kenny announced with much fanfare, "I'm afraid I must go out in search of sustenance. Would you like to accompany me or stay here and relax?"

"I'm with you," she answered, as she put only her loafers on and pretended to open the door.

Kenny laughed and rolled off the opposite side of the bed. "Personally, I'd love it if we could walk around like this. But I'm a bit familiar with the local laws and I'm afraid we wouldn't get far."

"That's really not a good color on you anyway," Samantha commented, gesturing to the sheet. "It makes you look drained."

"Honey, it has nothing to do with the fabric. Between operating on no food or sleep, yet putting out lots and lots of good loving, I'm a wreck!" The simple effort of making the statement made him fall back on the bed in defeat.

"Come on, you can do it," she encouraged, while untangling him from the linens. "I would love a nice Italian Dinner with a bottle of wine right now. Having my best fella next to me would just make the night, Hell, my life, complete."

"I think you are overrating me and the impact I have had on you, but hey, I'm not proud. I accept your challenge. Let's hit the bricks. It's late, but I know a few places and I still have a few surprises up my sleeve."

"Honey, I can see up your sleeve, as well as everywhere else and I don't think you could hide anything if your life depended on it!"

"Stop trying to seduce me!" Kenny snapped, before grabbing some clothes out of his suitcase and heading to the toilet.

She could hear him humming above the sound of the shower, while she put on some of the items from her new wardrobe. "What's that song that you always hum?" she yelled through the closed door.

"What?" he called back, "I can't hear you; come in here and talk to me."

"Never mind. I'll wait until you're done. No big deal." The thought of intruding on someone in the bathroom horrified her. Could there be any more personal a time? She didn't even like using the rest room at the office. Women going in groups to check their makeup and (God forbid talk between the stalls) confused her. What were these people thinking?

Kenny emerged from the bathroom with one towel casually thrown over his shoulders and another held around his waist. The latter was too small, so he was holding it tightly on his left hip and there was a wide gap exposing most of his thigh.

"Weren't you asking me something?" He directed to her reflection in the mirror, as he put both hands to his head and shook the towel vigorously back and forth, squeezing out the excess water from his hair. Of course this action meant losing his grip on the lower drape, but he didn't seem fazed by this at all.

"I didn't want to go in the bathroom with you-are you insane?" She looked at him as if he had told her to go ahead and walk outside naked.

"Why not, what difference does it make?" he asked in disbelief on his way back into the bathroom to retrieve the clothes he had already picked out.

"Because," she said slowly, emphasizing each syllable, "it's personal. I certainly don't want you in there with me, when the situation is reversed."

"You're joking! When I was growing up we didn't even close the door when we did our business, so to speak. Besides, once you've been in a gang shower with fifty football players, anything one on one is a treat!"

She stared at him, speechless. Finally he shook his head laughing and said, "Ok. No shared bathroom time. I get it, your majesty."

With amusement they both surveyed the room, which looked like a disaster area, before heading out for a walk around the town. It was a cool night, thankfully, and they were able to find a small restaurant that was still open within a quarter mile. It wasn't Italian, but at that point anything above rocks and mud would have sufficed.

It was during dessert that Kenny settled back in his chair with an espresso and a shot of sambucca to tell the tale of Piper's latest experiment. Samantha had forgotten all about the reference to Kenny's "real" father, as well as the brief discussion that had taken place after she had left his mother's apartments. She had to admit she was intrigued.

Only knowing the little she did of Piper, she was looking forward to this story. She settled back with her black coffee (sans liqueur) prepared to be amazed. And she was...

Chapter 53

Kenny took his time setting up the scene-bringing Samantha back to the visit with his mother. "As you can imagine, I was speechless by the time she pushed you out the door! My mind was racing so fast I couldn't figure out what to do first. I finally just collapsed onto the couch and waited for her to say something. The questions that were floating around: Who is my real father? Did Ryan know? Why didn't she tell me before? What could my father want from me at this point? Was my mother still having an affair with him? Believe me, that last one almost gave me a coronary!"

She tried to control her laughter, but she couldn't. It didn't take much imagination to picture the scene and she knew that Piper was only playing a ruse on her son, in order to teach him a lesson.

Kenny was smiling also, as he continued, "She didn't say a word, just kept staring at me with this look on her face that was driving me crazy. I started to scream at her 'Mother, you can't just drop a bomb like this and then clam up. What the hell are you talking about? I think I have a right to know.' I think her response to that was a very serious 'Really.' Not a question mind you-just a strong statement 'Really.' I started babbling like an idiot, 'Don't you know what this means? Everything I ever thought about myself is a lie. How am I supposed to deal with this? And you... you! What kind of a person are you to do something like this? I don't even know you anymore!" He paused to take a quick sip, while Samantha took a long, leisurely drink of coffee.

She stopped laughing, having a hunch where all this was leading. Part of her was sick to her stomach, yet another piece couldn't help but admire Piper even more for her incredible wisdom and understanding. Samantha had struggled for a long time, trying to come up with an explanation that would help Kenny see why the newly found note was such an important issue for her. Nothing made sense even to her, so how could she expect him to be patient, while she tried to sort everything out?

Kenny had continued talking and even though she had missed a lot of the story, it wasn't long before she felt back up to speed. "She then had the nerve to tell me that there was a reason I was named after the gardener (I didn't even attempt to go into the whole Kenny/Lenny charade)-are you ready for this? Because he was/is my real father! I don't know what upset me more, my mother betraying her husband or my real father having an affair with his employer who didn't even have the decency to know his real name!"

Samantha moved closer to him and stroked his sweaty temple. "Oh my poor baby," she said, again trying to keep a serious expression on her face.

Kenny's voice raised in exasperation, "I don't believe it-you already know how this ends, don't you? What did you two do, hatch this little scheme together?" He was only half joking, but he could tell from the hurt in her eyes that he was completely off the mark. "I'm sorry. I should have known better. My mother works alone! Anyway, I'm in utter torment and she starts peppering me with, 'What possible difference could this make in your life now? My God, you're a grown man-a brilliant lawyer with thousands of friends and not a worry in the world. So what if your father was a gardener instead of a hard working, self made millionaire, who just happened to marry an heiress. You are you and nothing can change that-ever.' I think I was careening around the room at this point, trying to illustrate in as many ways as possible how completely wrong she was. I told her it changed everything and I felt utterly powerless."

"She doesn't mess around with subtlety, does she?" Samantha asked quietly, a small smile returning to her lips.

"No, not at all. She then pretended to remember something, you know, even gave herself a smack aside her temple and said, 'Oh never mind. I'm mistaken. I guess Ryan was your father after all!' Of course I go nuts, asking her if she's trying to kill me and she calmly sits down and stares at me again with that look. A look that asked if I was the biggest idiot on the face of the planet. Finally, I stop blathering long enough for her to say, 'Don't be such a pompous ass. You seem to think that you would be affected to find out at this late date that reality, as you perceived it, was not the truth. Don't think for one second that Samantha won't be affected by that note, whether she decides to read it or not. It may absolve her of blame, it may blame her entirely or (God forbid) it may be a blank piece of paper. No matter what, there will be consequences, so get off your high horse and give her the support she needs to make the decision that is right for her and for the two of you.'"

Samantha's throat was closing in on her and she could feel the tears coming back, but she willed them to stay away. "I'll say it again," she said softly-leaning in to kiss Kenny, "she's quite a lady."

"I know. Sometimes I just need a jolt to remind me how incredible she is and how lucky I am to have her around."

"We all need a jolt now and then. Do you think you can handle another one so soon?" she questioned.

"I don't know. You might as well hit me with it; at least I'm still sitting. And hey-I've had a great meal, so if it is to be my last, I can live with that. Oops, no pun intended." Kenny laughed as Samantha rolled her eyes.

"I didn't bring the letter with me; however, if you are game, I'd like to open it when we get back to my house tomorrow."

"Are you sure?" he asked seriously, squeezing her hands in his. "I really do not want to pressure you. Believe me, I do get it now. Sometimes it takes awhile, but eventually I can be brought around."

"Thanks. And yes, I am sure. Now-let's enjoy the rest of our weekend and worry about tackling that when we get back. Right now I'd like to head back to the room and tackle you some more."

"CHECK PLEASE!" Kenny yelled, much to the other patrons' surprise. They paid with cash and were out the door as the desserts they ordered were being delivered.

They both sprinted loudly up the stairs on the return to the Inn and collapsed on the bed, breathing heavily from the unexpected exercise. But they weren't finished yet.

In the morning, neither one of them could move. They had spent the previous night using muscles they didn't even know they had. For the first time in a long time, they both were looking forward to getting into better shape...

Chapter 54

They checked out very late on Sunday, with many eyebrows raised throughout the Inn. Kenny was a familiar sight to almost everyone who worked there, but he seemed different with this partner. The parade of guests that they had seen with him before had been an eclectic mix of the most beautiful, young and sexy creatures the world had to offer. This woman was different. It had been obvious from the get go. They had an easy rapport that was infectious. She might make it back for a second visit and that made them happy for their friend. He finally found what he didn't even know he was looking for. It was rare for this to happen in life and not something to be looked on with disdain.

"Lucky bastards," was all that the bell hop whispered to his brother at the front desk when he returned from carrying the bags to Kenny's car.

"I know," was the only possible response.

Chapter 55

"I know you're anxious to get back," started Samantha when they had returned to the road, "but I'd really like to pop in on your Mother for about 10 seconds and thank her."

"Do you think that's wise?" asked Kenny, glancing over at her with a questioning look. "Things went so well, do we really want to give her another crack at you?" She noticed with unease that his face had taken on that look of distress that she had seen a few times before. The idea that he was still hiding something from her made her even more resolute with the idea of visiting his mother again today.

As quickly as the concern had appeared it was replaced with something else. "Tell you what. If you don't mind hoofing it from the corner, I could drop you off and then get gas down at Simmy's and swing by the studio to pick up a picture I left for framing. That wouldn't put us too far behind schedule and we'd both get what we wanted."

"And what is that?" she asked.

"You really want to see Piper today and I really, really don't!" he laughed.

"You're terrible," she said, while joining in with his laughter. "She's a dear and you don't know how lucky you are to have such a sweetheart, who loves you like she does."

"I am terrible, she is a dear, I do know how lucky I am and I realize she loves me," he ticked off responses to each of her points, "but once a month through the wringer for me, thanks anyway!"

He pulled the car over, as they reached the corner he had referred to earlier. "I'll have Hans come get you when I return, so you don't have to wait out on the street," he smiled, leaning over to kiss her on the forehead.

"Are you afraid your mother is watching from the window?" Samantha asked before unbuckling her seatbelt, pressing her body against his and thrusting her tongue into his unsuspecting mouth.

"Jesus, I'm just trying to make it to the gas station without a hard on, Sam. Can you give me a break?" He used both his arms to gently but firmly push her back towards the passenger side door. His expression indicated that he wasn't exactly displeased though.

"Ok, ok. I'm outta here. If it turns out this was a bad move, you know I'll blame you for not stopping me!"

He rolled his eyes, but she didn't see because she was already jogging lightly down the sidewalk with her back to him.

He pulled out into traffic and raised his hand in a wave as he raced past her.

Chapter 56

Piper handed Samantha a teacup and then sat down lightly next to her, patting her knee quickly with her hand. "I'm so glad that you came back to see me today, dear," she cooed, fluffing the pillows behind her back on the settee.

"I apologize for not calling first, but we were on our way back to Vermont, and I just felt a need to see you." She smiled shyly at Piper and continued. "I can't thank you enough for doing what I couldn't-I mean, what I had been unable to convey to Kenny, you just painted him the exact picture he had to see, in order to understand what I am going through." Samantha stopped, as Piper had closed her eyes and raised her hand, as if asking for silence.

"You don't have to explain any more to me, Samantha. I think I've intruded enough in your life for our first visit! You don't mind if I call you Samantha do you?"

She was unclear how to respond to this query. Did she mind being called her real name, instead of one that Piper had made up or misinterpreted? Was it a trick question?

Seeing her puzzled look, Piper elaborated. "Instead of Sam, that is. I noticed that Kenny called you Sam, so I wanted to make sure that I wasn't offending you by calling you Samantha."

After a sigh of relief, she responded, "Of course not. To tell you the truth, Kenny is the ONLY one that calls me Sam. Almost everyone else I know calls me Ms. Armstrong."

"That's sad," stated Piper, "you need to relax a little, child."

"Believe me, Kenny has been hard at work on that mission." The minute the words left her lips, she could have died from the embarrassment. She felt the color immediately rush to her cheeks and then tried to recover, which only made it worse. "I mean, he's good at distractions. Well, actually he's adept at taking your mind off you and concentrating on him-God that's not what I want to say either..." she faltered, as her voice trailed off.

Piper just stared at her with an amused expression. "You over think everything, don't you?" she asked.

"Amazingly enough, just where your son is concerned. On the job, I can't recall a time that I stumbled and sweat and blushed, like I do when I'm trying to impress that guy."

Her face softened and she returned her hand to Samantha's knee. "A little advice. Stop trying so hard. You did that the minute you met. He's hooked, so now you just have to make sure you don't let him go." Amusement was replaced with concern and again Samantha felt that Kenny and his mother shared some secret that had the potential of spelling disaster for the new lovers.

"Is there something that Kenny hasn't told me?" she questioned. When Piper turned her eyes toward the floor and didn't respond, she continued. "What is it? He hasn't lied about not being married, has he? I can take anything but that." Her eyes pleaded with Piper to answer.

"As far as I know, he has not lied to you. But he probably hasn't volunteered some information that you will eventually find out and could potentially find distressing. What I want you to do for me is to remember what you just told me. You said you could take anything but a marriage. I'm asking you to remember that."

"Mrs. Tucker, please—" she pleaded, "aren't there enough secrets in our lives as it is? Won't you tell me now, so we can deal with it and move on?"

"I can't. As much as Kenny would prefer that—" she paused to give it a chance to sink in that she and her son had discussed the matter of telling Samantha, "it's not my place. It wouldn't be fair to you, or Kenny, in the long run. Which is what I am hoping for here, Samantha. I think the two of you can have what Ryan and I had, but also so much more. And that isn't something you throw away. Not because of foolish pride. Remember that."

A knock at the door interrupted Samantha's train of thought. The man that had met her and Kenny yesterday for their visit and started to walk them down to Piper's room stuck his head into the sitting room. "Sorry to interrupt Mrs. Tucker, but Kenny asked me to bring Ms. Armstrong down to the front gate."

"Thank you, Armand. We were just finishing up." She turned to Samantha and held out both hands, indicating that she should be helped to a standing position.

After walking arm in arm to the door, Piper kissed Samantha on the cheek and gave her shoulders a squeeze. "Good luck, Samantha. With everything. I hope we can spend some more time together soon."

"I'd like that," she answered. "Thanks again for listening. And I'll keep in mind what we discussed. Goodbye."

"Goodbye, Samantha. Thank you."

Walking down the hall, Samantha stopped short. "I just realized something. You're Hans AND Armand, aren't you?"

The young man smiled and folded his arms across his chest before responding, "I suppose you could say that. My name is Hans, but Mrs. Tucker has always called me Armand."

"Doesn't that drive you crazy?"

"Not really. She's a tough old bird, but she's always been very good to me—" he smiled slyly and continued, "at Christmas, on my birthday, you name it. And Kenny has been great also. The two of them are something else."

"Let me ask you something. What do you think it means that she calls me Samantha?" After his questioning look, she added, "My real name."

"Well, let me put it this way. Other than her son, I'm not aware of anyone else that she hasn't, shall we say, renamed."

"So...?"

"So... I'd say that's either really, really good or—" Hans paused.

"Or really, really bad!" They exclaimed in unison.

They both laughed all the way back to the car. Kenny didn't say anything when she slipped inside beside him. He was afraid to ask...

Chapter 57

In contrast to the ride down, the return trip started out very subdued. Neither of them spoke much, both were introspective about the unknown that awaited them back in Burlington.

Now that Samantha had made the decision to read the note, Kenny wasn't as confident that this was a wise move. The little trick his mother played on him had made quite an impact while accomplishing its goal. His head ached from all the scenarios that were careening before his mind's eye, as he struggled to concentrate on the dull road that stretched out before him.

For her part, Samantha tried not to focus on the mysterious contents of the package; rather she chose to conjure up possible scenes that might follow its revelation. No matter what transpired, she didn't doubt that several things would take place: Kenny would be there for her, unwavering in his support; he would spend the night, but they would not make love (because of sheer exhaustion more than anything else); and she would experience-that term tossed around these days for everything-closure. It had taken her half a lifetime, but she was finally ready to put her mother's death behind her and start her own personal journey through the world. She smiled at the thought and turned to look at Kenny.

"Penny for your thoughts," he said quietly, without shifting in his seat.

"It'll cost you a Hell of a lot more than that, you cheapskate!" she exclaimed, glancing out her window in time to catch the sign that indicated they still had another two hours to go.

"Well it was worth a shot. Don't tell me, I don't care—" he began earnestly, but then playfully added "you secretive bitch!"

He waited until she looked over at him in disgust and then gave her a wink and a smile.

"Did you want to stop somewhere in Stowe for dinner?" she asked half-heartedly, hoping he wasn't counting on going anywhere but straight to her house.

"Not really. Did you?"

"Not at all. I don't even know why I mentioned it. Just wanted to hear your voice, I guess. The silence was starting to get on my nerves. How 'bout you?"

When he didn't answer, she pretended to knock on his temple while saying, "Hello? Anyone home? I said the silence was getting on my nerves. Can you help me out here with some meaningless chatter?"

"I'm sorry. I guess I thought if I could put all my energy into driving this car it would somehow speed up the trip. Is it my imagination, or does it seem like we left last week sometime?"

They both laughed; she turned in her seat, put her arms through his and snuggled close. "I'm sorry. Drive away, my friend, I won't bother you the rest of the trip. Just wake me up when we get home."

He smiled involuntarily hearing her refer to home. God he wanted to be at her house already and get this business taken care of. But he feared that there would be much more to it than that. It wouldn't be over tonight.

"Hey, no fair!" he shouted, jostling her awake.

"What do you mean?" she asked sleepily, trying to burrow her way back into the comfort of his body.

"I can't stay awake if you don't. Come on. Talk to me. I've got an idea. I've been meaning to ask you a few questions about something that I really don't understand," he said mysteriously, as she sat bolt upright.

She smoothed her hair, pushed it back from her face and gave a wide yawn. "A few questions about what?"

He gave her one of his most innocent smiles and said sweetly, "I know that your company is a captive insurance management firm; however, I've got to confess that I haven't a clue what that means. To save my life, I couldn't tell anyone what a captive is!"

Now she was fully awake. There wasn't a thing she hated less than talking about herself, yet not a thing she loved more than talking about her business. She was truly passionate about her work and Kenny couldn't help but laugh as she launched into a presentation designed to make everyone scream, "I want my own captive insurance company too!"

She stopped short, narrowing her eyes and asking, "You're not screwing with me, are you? You really want to hear this?"

"I really do," he said earnestly, again amazed at how naive and innocent she appeared.

"Ok. You are going to get the full treatment-from start to finish-since we have sooooo much time. Before we reach Burlington, you are going to be more of a captive expert than Carlene Dugan herself."

"I don't know lady, you're making some pretty hefty promises. Do you really think you can live up to all this hype?"

"You should know by now that nothing is hype about me, baby." She tried to be serious, but she collapsed into laughter.

"Come on, time's awasting. Let's get this show on the road!"

"Alright, let's see... where to begin. Well, with all good stories, let's start at the beginning. Back in the eighties," here she adopted the voice and demeanor of a very old woman, "some very wise men in the Vermont Insurance community were discussing why so many U.S. companies were setting up captive insurance companies offshore."

After observing a blank stare, she retreated positions and began again, "Captive insurance is formalized self insurance; therefore, a captive insurer is one that is started by a company to cover the risks of that company. Instead of paying premiums to a licensed, traditional insurance company, you pay those monies to your own company, you get the investment income on those funds and if you never have a loss, congratulations you have saved that money. Of course if you have claims, you need to pay those out of your own pocket, with the potential of having to pay more than you put into the company. But there are numerous ways to design a captive program, so you don't have to take too much risk."

"So where do you come in?" he asked, intrigued.

"Uh, uh, uh, I will be more than happy to answer any questions later in the program; however, I think if you just sit back and relax, you will find that most answers will be provided to you in the material I have prepared for your listening pleasure."

He grimaced, "So sorry, please continue. This is fascinating stuff."

She chose to ignore his eye roll, and went on enthusiastically, "Anyway, these types of companies had been around for years, but not a lot were domiciled in the States. And as I said, some savvy people in Vermont thought 'Can't we find a way to make this work here? Aren't we seeing a lot of good insurance dollars leaving the country for no reason?' So they put their heads together and crafted a really great law. The best, in fact. They made it possible for these companies to be licensed in Vermont-at a much lower capitalization requirement than some other states that had tried to introduce captives to their insurance departments-and to cover certain risks of their parents only. It just took off. These things have to be fully researched and controlled, i.e. not every company can (or should) do this. It is only in cases where it makes sense from a wide array of factors. Not all of which involve saving money, I might add. Maybe it is a vehicle that allows them greater control over their loss settlements and gives them stability over time regarding premium payments, instead of hopping from company to company each year based on who offers the lowest price. Maybe it is to cover business that they can't get coverage for elsewhere. Maybe it is to sit on top of a self-insurance program they already have or it might be the go between needed for them to access the reinsurance market directly. Every company I have is unique in the circumstances that brought it about, as well as the day to day operations."

She noticed his mouth opening and cut him off before he could ask his question again, "Ok, where do I come in? Each of these companies needs a Vermont Management Company to handle their affairs. We are the home office for the insurance company and all the books and records are maintained by us. The companies are audited and we have to prepare regulatory filings for the Vermont Insurance Department each year. Once every three years the Department sends examiners in to audit the CPAs and us. The captives have to meet in Vermont at least once per year and one member of the Board has to be a Vermont resident. Usually I perform that function; however, Carlene does it for a lot of her clients too.

Between the premium taxes generated off the business; the jobs created in the management companies, investment firms, law offices and accounting and actuarial areas; the tourism aspect, feeding off the meeting requirement; and the expertise built from all of the above, it hasn't been too shabby a deal for the old Green Mountain State."

Her mouth was dry from talking nonstop, but she was energized from her history lesson.

"I'm sold! I want one of these! Where do I sign?"

"Jest if you will, but that's basically the reaction I get after all my pitches to potential clients."

"I believe it," he said truthfully. It was obvious that she loved what she did for a living and he was jealous. He had never derived much pleasure from his work, only a sort of quiet satisfaction from doing a good job. Any resentment was quick to abate though, as he reminded himself how life has a tendency to balance out. His personal life had always brought him much joy and he knew that Samantha could never say that. He was happy that she had found something to compensate her for the pain of those early years.

"Guess what? We're back in Burlington, can you believe it?"

She was astonished to look out the window and realize that it was true. Talking about captives could always distract her from anything else that was going on.

Kenny took the exit for Shelburne Road and within ten minutes they were pulling up to her house. She was relieved to see the empty driveway, silently thanking God that Jeannie was not waiting for them.

"Let's just grab the bags," she suggested, jumping out of the car before it came to a complete stop and heading to the trunk.

"Not on your life, lady," Kenny said, reaching out his hand towards her. "Come on, we've got a note to read. Now."

He hadn't said it loudly, but firmly. She didn't waiver; she had made up her mind that too much time had passed already.

The note was on the dining room table. She sat down in one chair and pulled out the one next to it, indicating to Kenny that it was ok for him to sit as well.

"Good luck," Kenny whispered, as he gave her lips a light brush.

"You too," Samantha responded, starting to open the old, yellowed envelope with shaky fingers.

Chapter 58

Carefully she unfolded the contents; her fingers realizing that very thick stationary had given the illusion of more paper. In fact the note consisted of only a single sheet.

Samantha took a deep breath and tried to focus on the hand writing swimming on the page before her. She could feel Kenny beside her, more than likely finished before she had even started to read.

She skimmed the three lines, and then shaking her head in confusion, she reread them-with care this time. Kenny shifted in his seat uncomfortably, the look on his face a mirror to her own. "I don't under-what do you think this means?" she stammered.

"Should you read it aloud, maybe?" Kenny asked tentatively.

"Something isn't right about this," she murmured more to herself than to him, but she shrugged with annoyance and read:

> I don't expect you to understand, but please know that this was your mother's final decision. She didn't have a bad mother any more than you did. We'll all be better off this way.

Something was gnawing at Samantha, something deep down in her belly, but she couldn't put her finger on it.

Kenny gently reached up and took the paper from her shaking hand. "What odd wording, don't you think? And what's with the way she wrote her Ys and Fs-like the tails are backwards?"

"OH MY GOD!" Samantha gasped, as she jumped up and staggered around the room squeezing her head between her hands.

Kenny let the note fall to the floor. Roughly he grabbed her, hugging her to his chest tightly. "I am so sorry-what a stupid, stupid thing to say. I shouldn't have said anything."

When she didn't respond verbally, rather started to shake more violently, he took her face in his hands and screamed, "Jesus, Sam. What is it? You're scaring me. Talk to me!"

The look of horror on her face did nothing to calm his nerves. The tears were now cascading down her cheeks, as she tried to talk through her debilitating sobs. "That's it. That's what's wrong. My mother always had excellent penmanship-I remember now. All her photographs (from before she met my father) were labeled perfectly. Nanny told me that whenever people wanted something done nicely by hand, they would ask my mother to do it-even when she was a little girl. And my grandmother used to be so jealous! Of course. Oh God, what does this mean?"

Kenny was lost. He struggled with two conflicting ideas. Let her keep babbling until maybe it all became crystal clear to him, or slap her across the face in an attempt to get her to calm down before she started to hyperventilate. Her eyes pleaded with him to understand and some how help her make sense of the obviously devastating blow she had just received, but he couldn't find the words. "Well. She was under stress. Of course people don't act like themselves, when they are desperate to alleviate their pain—"

"No, no, no!" Samantha screamed, while forcing herself out of Kenny's protective arms. "Don't you see? My Grandmother is the one who writes like that. The note. Her Ys and Fs-she's the one that does that, not my mother. Nanny! My God, her own mother knew she was going to kill herself. She wrote that pathetic note-for God knows what reason-and then took me shopping!" She tried to control the spinning in her head; she fought against the feeling of traveling back in time. Her eyes were closed tightly, but still the scenes came spilling back. Her arms flailed about, in a futile attempt to get away from Kenny and back to her mother.

She could hear him in the distance calling, "You're ok. Take it easy. I'm right here. You'll be all right. Stay with me, Sam."

The arms that were holding her were transformed into a seat belt and she felt the familiar rock of her grandfather's truck as they descended the dirt driveway to their house. They were there again. Nanny's words came in her ears, "Jesus Christ, what are they doing here... today of all days?" She knew. Nanny knew what had happened in the house while they were gone. She had been part of it. She had not only let it happen, she had made sure it happened.

She was stumbling now and screaming as she made her way across the rock-strewn lawn. Inside the house there is hysterical shrieking. Oh it's happening again. There's Mommy dangling above her chair. And where is Nanny? That's right. She's searching for something. The note. The note that she knew had to be there, because she had been the one to write it. But it wasn't there, because Bud's mother had taken it. Why had she done that? Why didn't she tell anyone? After all these years, why did she give it to Samantha now? And what was she supposed to do with this newfound knowledge? Would the pain ever end?

I'm so tired. I can't think about it anymore. Time to rest. I'm in my bed, rocking myself to sleep on my knees, just like I used to do when I was a little girl. It's been so long. There. That's better. It's all going black...

Chapter 59

Kenny didn't say anymore, he just held Samantha loosely in his arms as she tried to work through the latest turn in events. He was frightened for her and himself. It was the overwhelming feeling of helplessness that frustrated him the most. There just wasn't anything he could do for her besides wait patiently. Not for a minute did he consider asking her to pretend that they never opened the envelope. He knew that it was too late for that. There could be no turning back at this point. He knew another trip to the Northeast Kingdom was on the horizon.

"I'm so tired," she whispered. It wasn't directed to Kenny, rather a statement she made simply for her own acknowledgement. After what seemed like hours, she finally felt capable of sitting up and facing him.

He smiled sweetly and held up his forefinger to her lips, when she started to speak. "I know. You want me to leave, so you can make arrangements at the office for being out a few more days. Then you have to pack, because you're driving to your grandmother's tomorrow."

She greeted his finger with a lengthy kiss before taking his hand in hers and holding it tightly to her chest. With her other hand, she traced the creases of concern covering his forehead and then tried to move a lock of hair that was dangling haphazardly over his eye. After three failures, she laughed quietly and fluffed up the offender that kept snapping back into his line of sight.

"I guess you think you know me pretty well, huh?"

"Yeah."

"Well I can't argue with you. That's it in a nutshell. I've got to get to the bottom of this once and for all. I want to move on with my life, but not until I have some answers. I've gone too far to stop now. I'm too close."

"I know. And I understand. Just don't forget to come back to me." He studied her through lowered lids, looking much younger than his advanced years.

She kissed him impulsively, gripping the back of his neck with a clenched fist. "I'm going to go out on a limb here," she said dramatically, clearing her throat. "Because you know me so well, you must know that I'll be back as soon as I can. I'll be back because I love–"

He knew how hard it was going to be for her to finish that sentence. In fact, he wasn't sure that he was ready to hear it. Even though he couldn't bring himself to say it either, it didn't mean that it was any less true. But there would be plenty of time for those words when all of this was behind them. When they were ready to start fresh with each other, with no secrets from their pasts between them.

"Hold that thought," he said softly, as he got up and kissed her on the forehead. "I'll let myself out. See you when you get back."

She simply nodded, unable to speak because of a large lump in her throat. When she heard his heels click across the kitchen floor, followed by the sound of the door to the garage opening, she jumped up and ran to catch up to him.

He was still in the doorway, with his back to her. "Be careful," was all he said, without turning to look at her again.

Samantha stood in the middle of the room, listening to the sound of his car backing out of the driveway. Beams from his headlights danced from ceiling to floor as he negotiated the potholes in the dirt road.

"Shit," she exclaimed, after glancing at her watch while jogging down the hall to her bedroom. There was so much to do and so little time. The walls seemed to be closing in on her, but she struggled to keep her breathing steady. Just keep telling yourself that the hard part is over, she pleaded silently. Pretend you are that naive for a few more hours. It has to be over by this time tomorrow night. There can't be any more questions-only answers at this point. No more surprises, please God.

She set out an outfit for the morning on the chair next to her bed and then threw a few more in her suitcase, just in case things didn't go as smoothly as expected. Poor Michaela would have to decipher her rambling voice mail message in the morning and continue to appease clients who must be starting to panic at this point.

After changing into a fresh pair of flannel pajamas, to combat the chill that suddenly enveloped the house, she snuggled under the high school graduation present that Nanny had made for her-a quilt that had covered her bed ever since.

She slept soundly. No dreams or nightmares, just blessed rest. She awoke before the alarm went off, feeling ready for the trip ahead.

The light was there at the end of the tunnel; she could sense it, even if she couldn't see it yet. Today would be the day to answer some of the questions she had carried with her for over thirty years. It was going to be a relief to be rid of the burden she had carried all this time. One way or another, the past would be put to rest. She wouldn't have to be tired anymore...

Chapter 60

Things were moving at a rapid pace now. She got on the road early, before the commuter traffic clogged her entrance to Shelburne Road. By briefly looking over her left shoulder, when she turned right onto Route 7, she was able to catch a glimpse of her office building. As expected, it was still veiled in darkness, waiting to be reborn with typical Monday morning activities.

She reached Montpelier in record time. The lights at the coffee shop beckoned, the smell of her favorite beverage wafting in on the cool breeze through the open window. Not wanting a dreaded caffeine withdrawal headache to kick in and destroy her good mood, she succumbed to temptation and pulled over.

The young girl at the counter was particularly curt with Samantha, but it was not something that came as a surprise. She was a stranger here, interrupting the morning rituals of the local regulars-such intrusions were not welcome.

After accepting her large black coffee with extravagant thanks, she put all the change from the five-dollar bill used for payment in the empty cup on the counter reserved for tips. It was worth it to see the expression of shock on the employee's face. Sam felt an urge to somehow let everyone know that she belonged there with them-that she wasn't some carpetbagger Flatlander, who had blown into town and stole a high paying job from a deserving Vermonter. There wasn't anything she could say, however, to change the cold reception she was receiving. From previous experience she knew that the minute the door closed behind her, they would all chuckle as the girl jingled her change and said, "Stupid rich bitch. Thinks she can buy us off with her spare change, eh? Who does she think she is, anyway?"

With a small amount of ironic satisfaction, Samantha looked in her rear view mirror and confirmed that the customers were in fact having a good laugh at her expense. She smiled. It was okay with her-today at least. She had bigger things to worry about, like pulling back out onto Route 2, when there was a small break in the traffic.

Within minutes of leaving downtown, the cars going in Samantha's direction were fewer and farther between. All the excitement was on the other side of the road, the dutiful public servants filing into the capital to conduct the work of the state. Each driver had a different expression on his or her face, so it was easy for Samantha to play her Grandfather's game of guessing who they were and where they were going.

She wondered what people thought as they looked across at her. Could anyone imagine anything close to reality? It was so easy to get caught up in the drama of one's own life. To think that your struggles are so much different and more important than anyone else's-your problems more complex than your neighbor's. Of all the travelers that she passed, who was going to visit a father in the hospital, a child at the police station, a friend who just lost her job? It was doubtful that anyone else was going to confront their grandmother about her role in her daughter's suicide three decades earlier, but that didn't mean that Samantha's mission was any more valuable than the others.

Contemplating such theories occupied her time through the long, lonely, winding roads between East Montpelier and St. Johnsbury. By the time she got to Elkin, the town was abuzz with children heading to school. Time and time again she was forced to stop at cross walks, as the stern, ancient-looking crossing guards directed herds of youngsters in front of her path.

Finally she was speeding past the Armstrong house, having decided the night before to forego another confrontation with her paternal grandmother. There would be nothing to gain from stopping and interrogating her about the reasons for keeping the note a secret all these years; she would save herself the agony.

As she got closer to the driveway of her childhood home, she was struck by how different the landscape was from her recollection. So much of the land had been clean cut; the thick beautiful trees of her youth only a distant memory now. The foliage was so thin that she could make out her grandmother's house from the highway, long before she had turned onto the dirt drive.

She took a semblance of comfort in the fact that no industry had sprung up on the route, the lone store she recalled from years ago, along with the only restaurant she ever remembered eating at as a child, were still unchanged sites less than a mile from the pond.

As she descended the steep grade, she noticed a new building to the left of the house. Getting closer she realized it was a two-car garage, something that her grandfather had always told her he was going to build someday. From the peeling paint, it looked as if he had managed to do just that, sometime during those four years when she away at college.

The house itself looked unchanged, along with the sparkling, black water that served as a backdrop. The gravel crunched under her tires, which would signal her grandmother that a guest had arrived. Samantha recalled the thrill that she had felt when she was small, upon hearing that sound. No matter where she was-in the house, down on the railroad tracks or swimming at the dock, she would come running as fast as her little legs could carry her. She smiled sadly to herself, realizing for the first time that she had always expected it to be her father. Of course it never had been.

After quickly drinking in the changes in the view across the water-an assortment of small cottages and large houses were built on top of each other, without a free strip of land that could be commandeered for a swimming area or boat launch anywhere-she turned off the engine and stepped outside her car. At least her grandparents had the foresight to buy the empty lots on both sides of their property, when they had gone up for sale in the early sixties. Samantha shuddered involuntarily just thinking about how much the land was now worth, yet knowing that it was more important to keep it undeveloped.

As she walked toward the front door, she placed her sunglasses on top of her head, preparing for the darkness that would greet her inside. She could only imagine the surprise that would register on her grandmother's face, after she made out who it was. She would probably be so thrilled to see her; she wouldn't even ask any questions about the last few "missing" years. On the other hand, perhaps Samantha was giving herself too much credit. Maybe she would not be greeted with enthusiasm, but rather disgust for the desertion that she had carried out.

She opened the screen door, pausing awkwardly with her hand shaking on the knob. This wasn't her home anymore, so she didn't feel comfortable just entering unannounced. She knocked three times loudly and then stood back to give her Grandmother lots of room to maneuver.

After several minutes of straining to hear sounds within and failing to, she knocked again and rang the doorbell this time as well. That immediately prompted a chair scraping across the kitchen floor and a weak voice responded, "Hold your horses, I'm coming!"

It was a shock when the door opened to reveal a stooped, arthritic woman who looked only vaguely like her grandmother.

"Yes?" she questioned, taking the time to survey the stranger from head to toe.

"Nanny, it's me. Samantha." It was all she could choke out as an overwhelming medicinal smell escaped from the cabin and enveloped her.

The eyes of the old woman narrowed, slowly absorbing the details of the words that she had heard, as well as the sight of the creature before her.

Just as Samantha was ready to turn and run for her vehicle, a broad smile broke out across the old woman's face and her arms extended to hug her errant granddaughter. Belying her appearance, her grip proved to be quite powerful. "See who's here, Sweetheart," she called back over her shoulder into the silent living room.

Samantha strained to see into the house, but instead found her face buried in wrinkled flesh. Other smells joined in to form a medley of offensive odors. She was able to separately identify rotting bananas and-was it-sour milk? In addition, it appeared that her grandmother was wearing a housecoat that Samantha recalled giving to her many years ago. It was safe to say that it hadn't been washed in quite some time.

If she had thought her father's mother had not been treated kindly by the years, what then, could she say about Nanny? Suddenly she had no idea what she hoped to accomplish and regretted coming. What could be gained by digging up the dead with this woman who looked more than ready to join her daughter and husband in the hereafter?

Samantha's mind was reeling, while her Grandmother pulled her into the kitchen and let the door slam behind them. As she had expected, it was dark and dreary inside, and the temperature was cooler by approximately twenty degrees. Her body was covered in goosebumps, but she tried desperately not to shake from the cold. Quickly she glanced around the room to verify that it was almost exactly the way she remembered it. Except for her grandmother's frail appearance, it was as if time had stood still waiting for her return.

"Let me look at you, child" her grandmother said, pushing her away from the embrace, yet not releasing her grasp. She shook her head back and forth slowly, clucking her teeth and then exclaimed, "Well you didn't turn out to be half as bad on the eyes as we expected, did you, Blossum?"

The bile rose in Samantha's throat. She wasn't sure if it was the use of her grandfather's nickname that upset her or the old feelings of ugliness and unworthiness resurfacing. Obviously Nanny had meant it as a compliment, but it served only to snap her back into the present and the task at hand.

"Do you want something to eat?"

"No, thank you. Nanny, I can't stay long, but I need to talk to you about something very important."

The smile faded from the older woman's face. "Honey, you just got here! Why are you talking about leaving already? That doesn't seem fair."

Samantha spoke over her shoulder while walking into the living room, "I know, Nanny. I'm sorry, but I've got to get back to Burling–" It was all she got out before the walls from the next room assaulted her.

Chapter 61

"Oh my God!" Samantha blurted out in horror. When she turned to look at Nanny, she was still there behind her, but the smile had returned to her lips and her eyes were twinkling.

"Surprise!" she exclaimed, clapping her hands in glee. "Pretty impressive, huh?"

Samantha was speechless as she slowly turned around in a circle, surveying the items that were literally papering the walls from floor to ceiling. Somehow her grandmother had gotten hold of every newspaper clipping that had ever mentioned Samantha, her company or the captive insurance industry and they were plastered to the structure, obscuring the natural pine panels underneath.

As she moved closer and studied the setup, she noticed that some of the articles were represented four or five times over. It couldn't have been any creepier if there was an altar complete with candles awaiting her on the pond side porch. "Nanny, what have you done?" she begged to know.

"It helps keep you close to me," she said simply, looking around and admiring her handiwork.

"But, why would you-where did all these come from?" Samantha asked incredulously.

"Everybody." Nanny responded with a shrug. "I must get twenty copies sent to me in the mail, every time you're in the Courier. Even that fancy business magazine over your way-people send me two or three of those too. To tell you the truth, honey, I've had to start throwing some of them away. I'm running out of room, if you can believe it." Since Samantha didn't respond, she continued, "Course I don't know what most of it means, but that don't matter. It's about my baby and that's all I care about. We're proud of you, Blossum. Damn proud. Ain't that right, Daddy?"

Samantha turned around expecting to see her grandfather and then sighed with resignation, slowly letting it sink in that her Grandmother had gone insane. Realizing how ridiculous it was to try and proceed, she nonetheless did just that.

"Nanny, please sit down for a moment. I need to talk to you about something. About someone... my mother."

Tears came to the woman's eyes as she pursed his lips and nervously ran her tongue over them several times before she spoke. "I was like a mother to you, wasn't I? Isn't that enough? Why do you want to bring her up after all these years?" She fell into a faded, ripped brown recliner, the springs groaning as she continuously repositioned herself in an effort to get comfortable.

Samantha grabbed a simple wooden chair from the dining set and pulled it in close to her grandmother. As much as it repulsed her, she took the cold, gnarled hands that were offered and squeezed them tight. "You were a mother to me and I will always be grateful for that. But I need some answers. I need to know about this." She removed the yellowed envelope from her sweater pocket and turned it to face her grandmother.

Her hands went limp; a low moan emitted from deep within her throat and the tears cascaded down her crinkled cheeks. Slowly she reached out to touch it. Tentatively she ran a forefinger back and forth across the letters written on the front. Her mouth opened and closed several times as she struggled to find the words she wanted. Finally, in a low even tone, she asked, "Where did you get this?"

When Samantha didn't answer quickly enough, she looked up and snarled loudly, "I asked you where you got this!"

"Grammy Armstrong gave it to me," Samantha answered deliberately, watching for any kind of reaction, "last week, after my father's funeral."

The tears stopped abruptly, and a nasty smile curled around her lips. "Yes, I heard about that. Sorry I didn't mention it to you earlier. I had prayed for his death for so long and hard-oh so long ago. Needless to say, it was a shock for me to hear that he had been alive and well, living right under my nose, for all these years."

Samantha didn't try to hold back the bitterness in her voice, "He was hardly well, but I guess that doesn't matter any more, does it?"

Her grandmother gave her a long, icy stare before responding, "It matters to me. It will always matter to me. That boy killed my girl and I will never, ever forgive or forget."

"It's so funny that you should say that," Samantha exclaimed as she got to her feet and turned her back on her grandmother. "When Grammy threw that note at me," here she turned to acknowledge the surprised look on her grandmother's face, "she said something about it being time for me to find out that my mother's death had very little to do with my father. In fact, she said I had you to thank for that."

"That wicked bitch!" Nanny spat, glaring at the note in her hands with a look that shot fire. "What the hell does she know about anything?" After a few more moments of silence, she collapsed into tears again, and clutched the envelope to her bosom as she rocked violently in the chair.

"I should have known that she took it that day. It was the only explanation that made sense. But how could she do such a thing? Why would she do it? Even for her that was a low blow."

Samantha reseated herself and attempted to get Nanny back under control. "I don't really care why she took it or why she held onto it all this time, Nanny, but I do care why you wrote it."

Color rose to her cheeks as she meekly answered, "I don't know what you're talking about. Why would I write my daughter's suicide note? That's just stupid."

Samantha smiled painfully through her tears. "But Nanny, you haven't even opened it yet. How do you know it's my mother's suicide note?"

The old woman's head fell back against the headrest, defeated. She was caught in a trap and didn't have the strength to try and fight her way out of it any longer. Samantha could almost see the thirty years of lies crashing down around her ears, could almost feel the crushing power of the truth strangling out what remaining life she had. She didn't feel sorry for her or regret her own actions that were bringing about this suffering. All she wanted was the rest of the story.

Without knowing why it mattered, she pressed on. "Tell me what really happened, Nanny. Please."

"What really happened..." she laughed eerily, "God, what does that mean? Where do I start?"

Samantha took her grandmother's hands with a steady grip, held her steely gaze and said, "Start from the beginning. Tell me everything, no matter how small and inconsequential it seems. Let me worry about whether it is important or not."

Nanny nodded, then her face brightened as she said, "At least you'll be here for awhile. There's a lot to tell!"

Samantha acknowledged this and then sat back to get comfortable, prepared to listen patiently to the whole saga.

Chapter 62

"I don't suppose you ever knew this, but my life started the way your mother's did. I was the prettiest girl in high school too, but my mother hadn't been a very good teacher. I didn't know how to use my looks to get ahead. I didn't know anything about boys, I just went from one day to the next having fun and not worrying about the consequences.

"When I found out I was pregnant, I was kind of happy at first." Samantha's sharp intake of breath was not lost on her grandmother, but she continued on without stopping. "My parents were devastated though. They wouldn't hear of me marrying John, although I know that's what he would have wanted, if he had known. But he was just a goof off in college, he had bad skin and his family wasn't anything special, so they wanted nothing to do with him. Your grandfather, who was an old family friend, happened to be in town for a few days before heading off for a tour in the Navy. He had always adored me and I was fond of him, so before we knew it, we were married. We never discussed the circumstances of your Mother's birth and I honestly couldn't tell you if he ever knew that he wasn't Miranda's real father or not."

Although Samantha hadn't counted on secrets being revealed prior to the day of her mother's suicide, she vowed to just listen to the story as told and ask questions later, if need be.

"I'm thirsty. I'm afraid I haven't talked this much in a long time, dear." She started to get out of her chair, but Samantha held up her hands to stop her.

"I'll get you a glass of water, Nanny. Please go on."

"Thank you, sweetheart," she said, as she settled back into the recliner. "Now where was I? Oh that's right. Your mother's birth. Everything went wonderfully, she was even three weeks late, which helped out with the timing problem, since it looked like she was only a little early. Anyway, she was the most beautiful baby there ever was," her voice choking in her throat and her eyes rewetting, "Yes, she was a beautiful, beautiful child."

Samantha handed her a tall glass of spring water and watched helplessly as she took a long drink before going on. It required all the strength she had in the world not to knock the tumbler out of her hands and scream, "Get to the point, old woman!" But she managed to hold her tongue.

"We were all very happy, you know?" Her eyes pleaded with Samantha to understand. Seeing no empathy, she still forged ahead, no longer looking at her granddaughter, instead focusing on the pond in the distance, through the windows of the porch.

"I couldn't have been happier. Your grandfather was thrilled with his little princess and your mother was such a confident, striking beauty. Even from the time she was a toddler, she could manipulate anyone into doing what she wanted. She was just that powerful."

Her grandmother's choice of words brought a sour taste to Samantha's mouth. There wasn't anything sweet and innocent about the word "manipulate". Still, she willed the judgmental thoughts to stay away until Nanny was done. It was all too much now anyway. Surreal. That was the word that came to mind. So much of her recent musings about her mother and father had been dreamlike-rather nightmarish. And yet this was just a natural extension of that alternate reality.

"She could have been anything. Well, not like you, of course." When Samantha cocked her head and looked at her inquiringly, she continued, "I mean, she could have married her way to the top. A doctor, lawyer, movie star, politician, tycoon, you name it. She wasn't smart like you, but it was a different time then. I did the best I could. Trained her to use what God had given her."

Her voice became louder, laced with bitterness. "But I didn't do a very good job because it wasn't long before HE came along and ruined everything!"

She seemed to be simmering in hateful thoughts, unable to continue, so Samantha prodded her with, "My father?"

"Yes," she hissed. "She thought she loved him and made a fool of herself inspite of everything I warned her about. He didn't love her! He just wanted a roll in the hay that he could brag about to his friends. He was going to dump her before he took off for college and I guarantee you that she never would have heard from him again." Her head fell into her hands, as if the memories were too much.

Samantha couldn't afford to let Nanny get off track now, so she selfishly pushed her forward. "If that's really how you felt, then why in God's name did you make them get married?"

Nanny looked up with what appeared to be amusement lightening her facial expression. "You can't possibly understand. I told you. It was a different time. Her life could have been ruined!" Samantha was amazed that her grandmother failed to note the irony of that comment.

"I guess in some small way, I was also trying to make it up to her real father. He hadn't been given the option of "doing the right thing" by me and I didn't want the secrets and lies to continue on to another generation."

She stopped to take another long sip of water and when she finished, she held the cold glass up to her cheek and stroked it gently back and forth as she continued. "You know it sounds so ridiculous now. I hear myself saying these things that I have practiced over in my mind for decades. Practicing all the time, so that when I finally spoke them out loud it would all make sense. But it doesn't, does it?" She didn't wait for a response. In fact, it was as if Samantha were no longer there.

Her grandmother struggled to get to her feet and then slowly shuffled across the floor and out onto the porch. She reached up for the venetian blind control-half closing them, allowing her to limit the amount of sunlight streaming in, but at the same time allowing the sight of the beautiful Green Mountains in the distance.

The porch was relatively unchanged from Samantha's recollection. She smiled as she felt the heat change when she followed Nanny from the frigid living room. This had been one of her favorite places growing up. She had lain on the old battered couch for hours reading-sweltering in the summer or freezing in the winter. It had made her feel close to her father after he left. It had smelled like him.

Samantha sighed with disappointment as she recalled the first time she had come across that smell as a grownup. It was in Hartford, when she passed the CPA exam. Her manager had taken all the rookies out to celebrate. She had looked around the room nervously, expecting to see her father, because the place smelled like him. But of course he was not there either. It wasn't exactly a unique odor. The place they went was a bar.

Chapter 63

For a fleeting moment, Samantha wondered if her Grandmother had plucked these "revelations" from thin air, in a mad attempt to keep her around. One confirming look at her pained countenance though erased that thought. The suicide note had opened the floodgates and now Samantha was going to get more truth than she could have ever imagined-certainly more than she had bargained for.

Samantha cleared her throat in an attempt to get control of her own emotions and also to reactivate her Grandmother's musings. "So my parents got married... when did it all start to go wrong?"

Nanny smiled sadly and shook her head slowly back and forth, exhaling loudly. "When had it been right? Bud was so resentful about having to give up college. As if your mother had it easier!"

Her grandmother plopped herself down on a ratty chair sitting askew, while Samantha leaned against the windowsill, looking outdoors. It wasn't that the view was so engrossing that she couldn't tear herself away-in fact, she couldn't even really say what she was looking at. She simply found it easier not to face Nanny anymore. And Nanny seemed to appreciate the break as well. The story flowed more rapidly now.

"I have never seen anyone get as ill during a pregnancy as Miranda did. Not without dying, that is. Hadn't seen it before-nor since." She rocked back and forth in the chair, clucking her tongue nervously. "She couldn't eat, sleep, read, watch television-nothin'. She just couldn't get comfortable. All those horrible stories about birth defects caused by the medicines that mothers were taking to feel better had just come out, so she wouldn't even listen when Johnny tried to give her something for the pain."

"Johnny?" Samantha asked, only mildly interested.

"Doc Bridges. As much as he hated me, he was always real fond of your Mama. Isn't that funny, though. Wouldn't you think that he'd hate her even more? Thinking she was your grandfather's daughter, of course. Not realizing the truth. Unless... I never thought of that before. Do you think he knew?"

Samantha's hands dropped from the blinds and she squinted as the pain in her temples returned. Slowly she turned to study her grandmother, before asking the question that was burning a hole in her brain.

"You can't mean that Dr. Bridges was your Johnny, as in my mother's real father?" The words were spit out, as if she could make the horrible taste in her mouth leave with them.

Nanny stopped rocking, a look of puzzlement appearing on her face. "What do YOU mean?"

Dropping to her knees, realizing too late that the carpet underneath had long ago lost any cushioning power, Samantha grabbed her grandmother's arm and shook violently while screaming, "Are you telling me that Dr. Bridges is really my Grandfather?"

"You're hurting me!" the woman cried out, slapping at Samantha's hands in a feeble attempt to dislodge her grip.

"I'm sorry, Nanny." Samantha loosened her hold, but did not move her face away and spoke clearly through the teeth she was grinding visciously together. "Just answer the question, please" she begged, "I don't know how much more of this I can stand!"

"Don't make me laugh!" Nanny exclaimed, the bitter look returning to her face. "You have no idea how much one person can stand. You'd be amazed."

Samantha lowered her head, trying to think of something to say that would jump-start her Grandmother's story again, but coming up with nothing, she remained quiet.

After several minutes, it was Nanny who broke the silence. "Yes." When Samantha acknowledged her with a few nods of her head, she continued. "Doc Bridges was my beloved Johnny. I guess our breakup was what he needed to get serious about his studies and thoughts of a career, because he turned completely around after that. I don't think we would have ever seen him again, if it hadn't been for his uncle's accident."

Samantha was so tired of having to prod her Grandmother at every turn, but for the sake of expediency, she faithfully played her part. "What accident?"

"Oh God, I don't even remember what it was. But his uncle was the only doctor in town back then, so when he was laid up, he needed someone to cover his practice. It just worked out that Johnny was going to be free for two months before he took a job out West somewhere, so he came back to help his uncle out. Of course two months turned into four, which turned into six and before we knew it, his uncle was retired living in Florida and Johnny was the only doctor in town. Of course he wasn't after awhile, but by then your mother had already started with all her problems, so she wouldn't hear of moving to a different doctor."

"I don't suppose anyone thought of bringing my mother to a psychiatrist at some point?" She struggled to get back to her feet and return to her perch towards the pond. "You know, for depression, or anything?"

She didn't turn around when she heard her Grandmother chuckling. The response was expected, "Humph. The only person who really needs a psychiatrist, is someone who would go to one in the first place!" Samantha couldn't argue with that old Vermonter logic. She herself had never gone to counseling. In college she had blamed it on her grandparents' initial refusal to allow it; however, she knew now that she shared that same stubborn streak with them. She didn't believe that talking to a stranger could be of any assistance in this department. And God knows you couldn't talk to someone you knew about such personal things.

But she wasn't upset anymore. She just looked at the woman in front of her-the woman who raised her-and wondered what difference any of this could make. Maybe everything she had just been told was true, maybe not. Maybe she just happened to be a baby in the hospital the same day that Samantha Armstrong was born. Maybe a nurse switched the bracelets, so instead of growing up as Caitlin Moloney, she had lived Samantha's life instead. Would finding that out now change anything? Does that mean no one is ever a whole person because they can't uncover every single lie that was ever told to them? Samantha no longer thought so.

I am who I am because of me-not others. And others are who they are because of them-not me. We may try to blame or absolve others, but it is all for naught. It just doesn't matter.

Samantha smiled as the air returned to her lungs that had been compressed for such a long time. She turned back to her Grandmother, holding out her hands to help her out of the rocking chair. "Come on, Nanny. I'm hungry. Let me take you out to dinner."

"Oh Samantha, no!" She said, looking in a mirror and smoothing her hair.

"Come on, I said. It will be fun. I bet you haven't been out of this house for months!"

Nanny laughed like a small child and pointed to her shabby dress. "I would hate to embarrass you, honey."

Samantha kissed the woman on her cheek and said softly, "You won't embarrass me, Nanny. If you want, we can go clothes shopping first. My treat!"

"Oh don't be foolish. I'll be back in a jiffy." She toddled off to the bedroom under the stairs. Samantha heard her rummaging around in drawers. After about fifteen minutes, she emerged wearing a lime green outfit. Samantha could tell it was new from the fold marks that were making rectangular boxes throughout the design of the dress. The bright red hat, with a black feather jauntily sticking out of it, made her appear as some sort of clownish Santa Claus, but Samantha didn't care.

She didn't even mind the strong smell of cologne emanating from her. In Nanny's haste to get ready, she had mistakenly grabbed some of her late husband's aftershave. Samantha took a long deep breath in of the fragrance and only let happy memories flood in as they got in her car and headed to the one restaurant that they both knew would be open.

The rest of the story that she came to get would come, but only after she gave her grandmother the one gift she wanted more than anything else-time. Time with the girl she had raised. A chance to see for herself what a fine job she had done. She could at least be proud of that, if nothing else in her life.

Chapter 64

They had a lovely meal together. Samantha didn't mind the stares or the bold people who came up to the table and made comments that were intended to be rude, but her grandmother took as compliments.

It was during dessert and coffee that Samantha heard the rest of the story. She hadn't prodded her grandmother; Nanny had just acquired a wistful look and started talking, while unseeingly looking to the distant corner of the room.

They all had known from the beginning that the marriage between Bud and Miranda wouldn't last. There wasn't enough of a foundation upon which to build a future. If it hadn't been for the pregnancy, Bud would have gone on to college and Miranda would have forgotten him within a few months.

"Your parents weren't strong people, Samantha. Not like you and me, at least. They were dreamers. And dreamers need people to protect them." Her eyes misted. "That was my fault. Not a day goes by that I don't regret being unable to protect your mother." She blew on her coffee and took a few tentative sips. "Yes. She told me she was going to kill herself. She asked me to keep you and your grandfather out of the house until final Jeopardy. Can you believe it? She actually planned it down to that. She loved that show. You and that show were the only things she cared about in the end. That day when she came back from seeing Johnny, we sat down and wrote the note together. Well, I wrote it, she just said it was okay."

Samantha's ears perked up and she dropped her coffee cup into her saucer loudly. "She saw Dr. Bridges the day she died?"

Nanny looked up startled, "Well, not that day, the day before. What difference does that make?"

Samantha's heart and mind were racing. After a few hours of thinking that nothing she could learn at this point could possibly matter, she wondered aloud, "I wonder what he said to her?"

"What? Oh, Johnny? He just told her that there was nothing wrong with her that medicine could fix. She was going to feel as miserable for the rest of her life, as she had those last few years. She didn't want to put any of us through that anymore. She decided she'd rather die and I respected her decision. I understood. Your grandfather wouldn't have, but I did. You do too, don't you?"

Samantha couldn't bring herself to agree, but she did say "It's okay, Nanny. Don't worry about it anymore." Secretly she was thinking that Dr. Bridges held the key to the last mystery. Surely he wouldn't have been so cold as to say what Nanny thought he said? She had noticed his house on Main Street, with his attached office, when she had traveled through town. My God, how old is he now, she wondered. He can't still be practicing, can he? You can bet I'll find out, she thought, as the last piece of banana cream pie made its way into her mouth.

She returned Nanny to the pond rather late, so she went in with her to make sure that she got changed into her nightgown and tucked into bed without incident. When she bent to kiss her on the forehead, she also gave her a hug and said with conviction that she would be back to visit her again soon.

Nanny had smiled happily and Samantha could tell from the rhythm of her breathing that by the time she reached the door, she had fallen into an exhausted sleep.

As she sped down the empty road into the black night, she vowed that she would just swing by Dr. Bridges' place to see if any lights were on; if not, she would go back to Burlington tonight, so that she could be with Kenny first thing in the morning.

Approaching Main Street, her heart skipped several beats as she noticed that only one house seemed to have activity inside. Dr. Bridges' house was brightly lit throughout. Exhaling forcefully to try and calm the butterflies in her stomach, she pulled her car into the parking lot and turned it off. The silence was deafening. She stepped onto the gravel and tried to close her door quietly, but the sound seemed to resonate through the whole neighborhood. A dog barked to the left-two cats started fighting to the right. Before she could be accused of causing more mayhem, she jogged up the front steps and rang the bell. There was a murmuring of voices from within. The porch spotlight clicked on-blinding Samantha, and then the door was pulled open.

Chapter 65

It took Samantha a few minutes to adjust her eyes and see that she was face to face with a very angry, elderly woman. "What do YOU want?" she snapped.

"I'm terribly sorry to bother you, but I saw your lights and I was hoping to speak to Dr. Bridges-just for a moment." She added the last part quickly, after noticing the look of disgust growing.

"I'm from Burlington" she stammered, "and heading back there right now, in fact. Otherwise, I wouldn't have bothered to stop. I mean, tonight, but it's important. But like I said, I'll only take a few minutes." Oh God, what am I doing, she wondered, hoping something would fall out of the sky and knock her unconscious.

"Mother?" a voice called from behind and above the woman.

Samantha saw a staircase along the left side of the wall, which curved to the right when it reached the next floor. She noticed a pair of legs jogging down the carpeted center, at the same time the woman turned, holding the door open wider for a man to join them.

"I'm Dr. Bridges, can I help you?" the handsome man, who looked vaguely familiar, asked. A look of surprise came over his inquiring expression as he continued, "Please come in."

Samantha obeyed, surveying the man who must be a few years her junior. "Oh, I'm sorry. I guess I am looking for your father? Dr. John Bridges?"

"My husband is dead," the woman spat, as who Samantha assumed was the son closed the door behind her.

"Oh. I'm so sorry. I should have known. I won't bother you any longer."

"It's alright," the man said more to his mother, than to Samantha. He pointed up the stairs while explaining, "I'm Dr. John Bridges, Jr. I took over my father's practice about six months ago. Perhaps there is something I can help you with? Please, come up to my office and we'll see what I can do."

"J.J.?" The woman seemed frightened at the proposal.

"Just a minute, Mother, let me get Ms. Armstrong settled and then we can have a few words." He took Samantha's arm and directed her to the stairs. She climbed obediently and when they reached the second floor, he pointed to an open door where a desk and lit lamp were visible. "Please, make yourself comfortable-I'll be right back."

Samantha removed her coat and draped it over the chair that was placed in front of the desk. She heard a door slam from below and then voices arguing. She couldn't hear what they were saying, just the general idea that Dr. Bridges was trying to explain something calmly to his hysterical mother. She fought the urge to run back to her car and instead focused on reading the citations adorning the walls of the small room.

All of the items belonged to the father, not the son, and were rather old and outdated. She sat down in the chair, realizing that the voices had quieted and she could hear someone padding back up the steps. Dr. Bridges held up his hand when she attempted to rise upon his entrance, insisting that she stay seated.

"So, what can I do for you Ms. Armstrong?" he inquired, his dark eyes flashing with, what was that she saw-fear?

"Well, first of all, I must apologize. You seem to know who I am, but I don't recall having the pleasure—"

He cut her off with a laugh. "Everyone in this town knows who you are, Ms. Armstrong."

"Please, call me Sam," she offered, startled to hear herself say the nickname that she only let Kenny use. For some reason she felt comfortable with this stranger, perhaps it was his familiar look. Maybe she did know him? It was then that she realized with a start that she was focusing her attention to his mouth. He had her mother's mouth. That was it. Of course! He was John Bridges' son. That meant he was her uncle!

He had continued talking the entire time she had been daydreaming; she listened as he recounted various achievements that had obviously been reported in the local news. She squirmed uncomfortably in her chair, trying to come up with an opening to her query.

"Sam it is then. Now, how can I help you?"

"Well I don't know that you can, actually. I don't even know why I'm here. I've just recently been going over some details of my mother's death-I don't know if you are familiar with that?" her voice trailed off and she looked at him through lowered lashes.

"I, uh, heard about it. Not from my father, of course, but I guess you would say, around? I'm sorry."

His peculiar choice of words was setting off red flags; nevertheless, she plunged forward. "Your Dad was her doctor and I found out today that he had seen her the day before she committed suicide, so I was hoping to talk to him and see if there was anything said that might explain WHY she did what she did."

After a long pause, he answered "That was a long time ago."

"I know and it's probably stupid, but I just thought it would be worth it to ask."

"I'm sorry that I can't help you, except to say that if my father had known anything, he certainly would have been obligated to come forward at the time it happened."

Again, the odd choice of words. Not, he would have come forward, but he would have been obligated to. J.J. seemed to be under duress. What was he hiding? Did he know that Miranda was his sister? Was Samantha just imagining all this? "I just thought that if maybe you could look at her records, there might be a reason buried in there somewhere. Why she felt that everything was so hopeless."

"No!" He jumped out of his chair and ran his fingers through his thick salt and pepper hair. Samantha grabbed her chest, startled by his outburst.

"I'm sorry," he said quietly, "I just meant, that it's impossible. Unfortunately, all of my father's records perished in the fire."

Samantha's eyes grew wide as he continued. "My father used to work late at night. Even later than me." He chuckled, pointing around the room and to the moon out the window above his desk.

"He also had the filthy habit of smoking. Can you imagine, a doctor for almost fifty years?" He sat back down at his desk, propping himself up by his elbows, gazing at Samantha with a strained expression. "One night, he fell asleep-smoking. Before my mother could get to him, the whole south section of the house, the practice area, was engulfed in flames."

That's why this didn't look familiar, she thought. When she had gone to Dr. Bridges as a child, her grandfather she thought with melancholy, it was at the end of the house opposite from where they sat now. "I'm sorry, I didn't know."

"I'm sorry that I can't help you. Any physical records were destroyed in the fire. And any mental records died with my father. He never had any partners. Never shared anything with my mother either." The last part was added quickly and rather loudly.

Samantha took a chance on finding out if he knew the truth about their connection, by asking him point blank, "Do you have any brothers or sisters, Dr.?"

He seemed surprised by her question, but he didn't hesitate when he answered, "No. My parents were late bloomers. By the time they had me, that was all she wrote." He laughed and Samantha knew without a doubt that he was unaware of his half sister. She decided that he would never hear it from her.

"I'm an only child too. Just like to see how many of us there are out there."

He accepted her weak attempt at an explanation without question and then she got up to leave. She extended her hand and thanked him for his time. "Again, I apologize for disturbing you and your mother. Please let her know how sorry I am."

He nodded his head as they returned to the first floor together. She waved to him one last time from her car; he stood on the porch for a long while watching her drive away. Then he slowly went back inside. He told his mother that everything was fine before he headed back upstairs to his makeshift office.

She had been on a fishing expedition, he thought, but with no idea what she was looking for. He didn't suspect that she would return; however, there wasn't any point in leaving anything for her to find, should she make her way back.

He locked the door behind him, then unlocked the top left-hand drawer to the old oak desk. He carefully pulled the shabby leather bound journal from its hiding place and read it one last time before throwing it in the fireplace to burn with the rest of the logs. It was the only record of his father's that had survived, because he had purposely left it on his wife's nightstand before going back to deliberately set the fire.

J.J. tried to understand why his father had done what he did, but he didn't recognize the man who wrote his thoughts in that book. He couldn't identify with the heart broken soul who had returned from college for vacation to find that the love of his life had married someone else. He couldn't feel the depths of his depression when he learned that a mere nine months later they were the proud parents of a beautiful baby girl. John Bridges had filled a book with his life long obsession of Catherine Atherton. How everything he did for eighteen years was to impress her. Then how his goal changed to hurting her as badly as she had hurt him.

He recounted how close he had gotten to Miranda Armstrong, until one day he had broken down and told her how much he hated her mother, the woman who had scorned him. Miranda had surprised him by commiserating, spending long appointments telling him about how that woman had ruined her life as well.

He wrote how it had saddened him the day he received the test results back. To have to tell Miranda that she had an inoperable brain tumor that would kill her within two months was the hardest thing he had ever had to do. It had been her idea to keep it a secret. She wanted to kill herself, after telling her mother that she was going to do it. She wanted her mother to have to live with that the rest of her miserable life. He wanted that too. He wanted her to suffer the loss of the daughter that she loved so much. So he told no one. No autopsy had been performed. Everyone knew the history of Miranda's depression, so no one suspected anything else.

Everything had been fine until Bud died. Bridges wrote in his confession that he had surreptitiously gone to the funeral, so that he could see Miranda's daughter. Something snapped inside him when the enormity of what he had done all those years ago hit him full force. He had wanted to tell her the truth about her mother, but his reputation would have been ruined, his wife and son devastated if any of this came to light. So he took the only way out that he could. He left the journal, so that J.J. and Joan would know why he had always treated them aloofly. Maybe by admitting his selfishness, they could find some sort of peace and move on with their lives before it was too late.

J.J. vowed that this would be the end of it. He couldn't bring his father back or relive their time together differently, but he wasn't going to let it ruin his life too. He would tell his mother about burning the journal later. She was too upset right now.

*

In another part of the house, Joan was fuming. She was very bitter. She couldn't understand J.J.'s compassion for that girl, but she knew she hated Catherine Atherton with every fiber of her being. When she had seen Samantha on her doorstep that night, she had hated her too. But there was something else. She cried for herself and her son now, for they had endured a loveless life with her husband. But she also cried for that man, who had never known the truth. It had come to her immediately upon opening the door, because she had seen it in the mouth as well. She had seen her husband's features in that girl. She had realized what his hatred had not allowed him to see all those years ago. She knew that Miranda had been his daughter. So she cried for the father and daughter who had committed suicide over thirty years apart. And she prayed that this would be the end of everyone's pain.

Chapter 66

It was done. Over. There was nothing else to do but get on with her life. She was ready for that. Now. The car could not go fast enough. With all her might, she willed that the miles would melt away between Elkin and Burlington.

She thought of Kenny the entire time, the road twisting and turning before her. A few times the wheels seemed to leap off the pavement at sharp turns, sending enough fear coursing through her veins to slow her down for a few minutes at a time.

Traffic was heavy, so she didn't have the usual lonely feeling of being a sole traveler in the middle of nowhere. She smiled as people passed her on the interstate-nodding politely, letting them assume that their destination was more important than hers.

She hadn't quite made it home before realizing that she couldn't wait until morning to see him. His house was across town, but it wouldn't be more than a few minutes before she could be in his warm, strong arms. Speeding up as she went by the turn for her street, she was getting horny just at the thought of seeing him.

His neighborhood had gone through a generational cycle of being the ritzy part of town that eventually fell in to disfavor and ruin, until it was rediscovered by Yuppies who bought up all the dilapidated property for a song and then rebuilt it. She knew she had the right lane, but since she had never actually visited, she had to peer through the darkness at the numbers painted on the mailboxes and count softly to herself, looking for 101.

This must be it, she cried triumphantly, until her heart fell upon the sight of a familiar car in the driveway. Yes, Kenny's sportscar was next to the garage, but parked directly behind his was another car. Normally, it would have been at her house, but things had gone haywire in her life lately, so nothing was as it should be.

She tried to remain calm as her shaky hand knocked softly on the front door. Again the feeling of despair in her stomach that she knew all too well. She thought all the questions had been answered, but she was about to go another round. Why in God's name is Jeannie at Kenny's house? she wondered, as the porch light came on and the door was pulled open...

Chapter 67

"I can get my own God damn door," Kenny yelled over his shoulder, as he yanked hard at the swollen portal. Samantha's hopes were dashed as she heard the feminine laughter in the background.

"Sam!" he exclaimed, relief flooding his face. She was startled when he took her into his arms and hugged her close to his body. He smelled so good. "I'm so glad you're back. How was your trip?"

Her expression had not changed since seeing Jeannie's car. She glared at him with distaste, challenging him with her eyes to make this terrible nightmare go away.

"Ohhhhhh," he stuttered, looking back into his living room and then again to Samantha. "I'm not going to make the mistake of saying, 'I can explain' or 'It's not what you think'. I'm just going to ask you to trust me and come inside. You're shivering. Come on."

He was able to pull her across the threshold, despite the resistance she was offering. Her body was rigid-her mind shutting down in an attempt at self-preservation. The eerie feeling that had come over her that first time that Jeannie and Kenny had met at her house returned. Apparently they did have a history together. A relationship that she was not eager to delve into. She didn't want to hear anything that they had to say. She couldn't keep fighting these battles, trying to uncover everyone's secrets. It was too tiring. It took too much out of her. She couldn't do it anymore.

"I'm going home, Kenny," she whispered.

"You can't, Sammy. The fun is ready to start. Wouldn't you say so, Ginger?" It was Jeannie's voice. Samantha looked over and saw the broad smile on her face, even though the eyes were filled with hate.

"Don't ever speak to me again," Samantha spat in Jeannie's direction, although she was studying the young woman sitting next to her on a barstool. Ginger, was it? Very striking beauty. What role did she play in this sad affair?

"Ginger?" It was Kenny's strained voice that made them all turn their attention back to the front door. For the first time since she arrived, Samantha noticed his drawn features. She wanted to run to him, bury her face in his sweater, as she stroked his head and tell him that they could work it out, whatever it was. But her pride wouldn't let her budge. Not until she knew the whole story. It might cost them their relationship, but at this point she had no intention of accepting anything less than a clean slate.

Kenny clasped and unclasped his hands nervously, as he worked through in his mind exactly what he wanted to ask. He closed his eyes tightly for a few seconds, took a deep breath and then beseeched Ginger; "Please... I am begging you... tell Jeannie to get the Hell out of here. This is between Samantha, me and you-only."

Jeannie laughed and went into the kitchen, as Ginger sat quietly looking at Samantha. They heard the refrigerator door open and close, followed by the hiss of a beer being opened. She returned with a half empty bottle in her hand, kicked her shoes off and settled on the couch, after a very loud burp.

"Oh that's classic," Samantha said to no one in particular, as she made her way to the door.

Kenny blocked the exit with his arm and yelled once more, "Ginger? Please?"

Jeannie's giggles were cut off this time by her friend. "Hit the bricks, Jee. I'll meet you at Diane's place later."

"No way, Ginger. I've been waiting a long time for this and I'm not going to miss it for anything in the world." She drained the rest of her beer and dramatically placed the empty bottle on the coffee table. Next she proceeded to knock it over, when she swung both feet up from the floor.

"You're an idiot," Ginger said, slapping Jeannie's arms and legs while gesturing to the door. "Now that I see them together, I realize this isn't some big joke. This is serious."

Jeannie was on her feet now, trying to gather her belongings as Ginger continued to herd her out. "I will never forget this, Ginger! Make no mistake about it. You have no idea how nasty I can get—"

Kenny moved aside to let Jeannie pass, all the while clinging to Samantha's jacket. She could have easily slipped out of it and been on her way, but curiosity had hooked her. She needed to hear what Kenny and this nymph had to say.

The silence after Jeannie's departure hung uncomfortably in the air among the three of them. Ginger smiled at Samantha and shrugged. Samantha walked towards her with an extended hand and introduced herself awkwardly.

Kenny looked every bit his age, as he left his post at the door and joined the women in the living room. He indicated the couch and then perched opposite on the arm of a recliner.

"I do know how weird this is for both of you and I apologize. If I could just have a few moments of your time, I'll try to explain how we got here."

Both Ginger and Samantha looked at each other briefly, before nodding their acceptance.

"First let me say that I do realize what a selfish bastard I have been. I am so sorry. I never meant to hurt either one of you, but I know that's not much consolation." He turned to Samantha and said, "The morning of the day we met, I had bought an engagement ring with the intention of asking Ginger to marry me that night."

The statement cut through her heart like a knife. She couldn't remember anything that she had previously suspected he might say. Nothing like this. It was totally unexpected. Her hand had involuntarily gone to her mouth-her thumb and forefinger were covering her nostrils, making it difficult for her to breath. Forcefully, she exhaled, trying to get her heartbeat under control. She could feel Ginger fidgeting next to her, but she couldn't look at her. Not yet.

Kenny tentatively reached out to touch her knee, but changed his mind and withdrew his hand. He turned his attention to Ginger. "I thought I wanted kids more than anything else in the world. I was panicking that time was running out. I'm sorry that I could have thought for one minute that getting married was a good idea. It wasn't fair to you. I hope you can forgive me. Some day."

Samantha got to her feet. "So what you're saying is, you panicked and bought an engagement ring for this woman. Then that made you panic, so when you happened to meet me later that day, you conveniently fell for me. But that was just an excuse to get out of an uncomfortable situation. That you put yourself in, in the first place!"

"No! That's not it at all." He grabbed her arms, nothing tentative about his reach this time. "I guess what I'm trying to say is that I had been focused on an outcome for so long, that I forgot that sometimes the most important part of the process is the journey along the way. It's when I stopped looking for those few hours that you just fell into my life. Nothing has ever seemed that easy, that right, to me. Ever. I love you, Samantha. It's that simple." He let his arms fall and he collapsed into the recliner.

She looked down at Ginger, who was quietly wiping tears from her eyes. Her heart ached, but she didn't know if it was for herself or the young girl beside her. He had said the words that Samantha had longed to hear her whole life and she desperately wanted to say the same to him. But what did that mean? They wanted different things from each other. It could never work out. It was too late.

"Goodbye, Kenny. I'm sorry, Ginger." She felt the hot tears stinging her eyes as she reached for the door handle, but there was rustling behind her.

"Wait!" It was Ginger who had gotten up and quickly rushed behind her, not Kenny. "You're not walking out on him, are you?"

"What? What do you mean?" Samantha stammered, wondering how this young, gorgeous creature could sit there listening to her would-be fiancé's confession about loving another woman and then try to play matchmaker.

"Look. I don't pretend to understand it all myself, but I've got to say that you're a fool, if you're going to throw him away because of me. Me and Jeannie." She laughed nervously. "She really is an asshole, you know. You spoiled her rotten, but she was too self centered to appreciate it."

"I don't give a shit about Jeannie-or him," Samantha said without much conviction, inclining her head towards the living room where Kenny sat with his head in his hands.

"You're lying," Ginger stated.

"Why do you care?" Samantha asked incredulously. "Hasn't he hurt you enough?"

"You know what? I'm not that hurt. I'm embarrassed, but that's my own fault. My big mouth friend told me when Kenny bought the ring and I called everyone I knew. I'm not proud to admit this, but I was more interested in marrying a rich lawyer, than making Kenny happy by having a bunch of kids."

"Well I don't want any children. I never have. So being with me isn't going to work for him either, is it?"

At this point Kenny rose from his chair and slowly walked toward them. "Could I jump in here for a moment? Has anyone been listening to me? I can live without children, but I can't live without you. I need you. I *LOVE* YOU."

Samantha studied his face for a long time before responding. She turned to Ginger and said, "I think he means it."

Ginger laughed softly, the tears flowing down her cheeks. "I know he does. In all the time we were together, he could never say it to me. I'm gonna leave now. You two do me a favor and work it out, ok? They say June is the perfect month for a wedding." She picked up a jacket that lay on a shelf by the door and let herself out.

They both stood silently staring at the floor shuffling their feet. Finally Samantha broke the silence. "You could have told me you know."

Kenny looked up and smiled. "I know. There were enough opportunities. When you asked if I was married. When I knew that I couldn't marry anyone else. When you pressed up against the ring box in my pocket—"

Samantha gasped, "Oh my God! That's what that was? At my house? That first morning?"

"I know. It sounds so horrible," he said sheepishly. "But you have to give me credit, I did try to tell you on the way to my mother's and you said it didn't matter!"

"Well that's when I thought it was ancient history-not the ring receipt was still in your wallet!"

"Ok, Ok. I'm sorry. I'm an idiot. But an idiot who does love you very much. So much it hurts. I mean it. If you'd agree, I'd marry you tomorrow. Or?????"

They both looked at their watches and said at the same time, "Today!"

Epilogue

Kenny and Samantha were married in the middle of June at Bowtie Bay, with one mother and one grandmother in attendance. After much protesting, both Piper and Nanny agreed to spend the summer with the newlyweds-but only after they returned from a three-week honeymoon.

It had been Kenny's idea to stop in and visit Mark Monahan, when they drove by the exit for his company on their way back from New York.

Although Mark seemed truly happy for them, Samantha and Kenny had to wonder exactly how miffed he was at being excluded from the private ceremony-especially when he suggested lunch at the cafeteria downstairs.

The reason became all too apparent when his son, Trevor, waited on them. Samantha was as pleased to see him, as he was irritated. After they were seated and eating, their host raised his glass and offered this toast to the couple: "Give your love freely to your children, because you can never love them too much. Hold back on the material items though, because despite what you think, you will never give too little. May you never know the pain of raising a spoiled rotten Harvard Graduate, who won't move out of your house and refuses to get a real job!"

Kenny blushed and concentrated on running his napkin over the table in front of him, but looked up when he heard Samantha laugh.

"Oh Mark! Thank you so much for everything. Believe me, we'll keep that in mind *and* put it into practice shortly." She rose and gave him a long lasting hug, before looking down and winking at her husband.

"Sam? I thought... Well I didn't think..." Kenny stammered, unable to get his tongue to form the words he wanted.

"I didn't think either. But people can change, Kenny. And I have. I feel like the second luckiest person in the world!"

"Second luckiest?"

"Yes. The way I figure it, our baby has got to be the luckiest with you as a Dad." She squealed with delight as he jumped up from the table, wrapped his arms around her back and lifted her to him. All the time wearing the widest grin she had ever seen on anyone's face.

About the Author

Patricia Letourneau Henderson grew up in the Northeast Kingdom of Vermont, before heading off to Keuka College in the Finger Lakes Region of New York. After graduating with a B.S. in Business Administration-Management, she moved to Boston for a three and half year stint as an Accountant with Liberty Mutual Insurance. Returning to Vermont as a Captive Insurance Company Manager, she has spent fifteen years in the business. Currently she is Director - Corporate Services and Vermont Operations for Strategic Risk Solutions in Burlington.

Ms. Henderson, her husband and two children divide their time between homes in North Concord and Essex, VT. She welcomes your questions and comments at captivebooks@aol.com.

Printed in the United States
823700003B